The inexorable course of love...

Bending a little, Mike picked Joy up without much effort and carried her to his bedroom. He stood her on her feet and reached to pull the shirt off over her head. Joy was still, looking into his dark eyes, then put her hand to his shirtfront, unbuttoning it, concentrating to keep her mind from telling her she could still stop her straight path to destruction.

He finished undressing her, and she waited as his eyes went over her figure. Mike brought her close to him and whispered her name. She slid her hand along his hip, hesitating. She made a quick move to withdraw from his arms, but he held her.

"No, darling. You can't leave me now."

ABOUT THE AUTHOR

Zelma Orr had a most interesting career before turning to writing full-time. She was a U.S. Customs Officer for the Treasury Department in her home state of Texas. Zelma loves to travel and keeps a diary of the places she has visited to use for backgrounds in future books.

Books by Zelma Orr

From This Day

ZELMA ORR

Harlequin Books

TORONTO • NEW YORK • LONDON
AMSTERDAM • PARIS • SYDNEY • HAMBURG
STOCKHOLM • ATHENS • TOKYO • MILAN

Published July 1985

First printing May 1985

ISBN 0-373-16111-5

Printed in Canada

Chapter One

Joy Strayer drove through the December traffic without thinking. She hadn't done much thinking at all that morning, what with walking in a fog, which had nothing to do with weather.

There was nothing she could put her finger on; she just felt useless and out of sorts. Not that those feelings were anything new lately, she went on thinking as she slowed for the next light.

Brushing the heavy black hair from her face, Joy's fingers touched her cheek. She frowned. Although she felt cold, with the heater not yet warming the car, her face was hot. Moving her head from side to side to ease the stiffness in her neck, she grimaced as an annoying pain started at the base of her skull. She was never sick, and this near Christmas wasn't the time to start.

At North Virginia Avenue she stopped for a red light and noticed for the first time the swirling snowflakes falling steadily between her car and the one in front of her.

I hope it snows enough to make everything pretty and white and Christmassy-looking, she thought, feeling drowsy and sluggish. Christmas was her favorite holiday, and she got as excited as the kids pressing their noses against store windows to stare in fascination at the bright decorations, with toys packaged in tempting array.

The raucous sound of horns blowing irritated her, and her head throbbed in time to the noise. As far as she could see, there was nothing to cause such a commotion, and she sat huddled in her coat, trying to keep warm. The heater must have stopped working completely. The snow enclosed her in a private little space broken only by the slight nagging pain in her neck and an impatience to get out of the traffic and to her office.

A tap on the glass made her turn to see a policeman stooping to look in the car window. She rolled it down.

"Are you stalled, ma'am?" he asked politely, indicating the traffic her car was blocking.

She stared into the face so close to hers. It moved away, becoming blank, without features, then came back into focus.

"I—I—" Her voice cracked, and she put her hand up to push the hair from her hot forehead. For the moment, she neither knew nor cared where she was, and surely, the cars could go around her if she was in their way.

The officer's lips tightened, and he opened the car door. "Slide over and I'll move your car out of the traffic."

Obediently she slid from beneath the wheel across the seat to the passenger side, and as the policeman parked the car by the curb, he turned to look at her, dark gray eyes accusing as they went over her tumbled hair almost covering her wide blue eyes.

"Have you been drinking?" he asked, his voice decidedly unfriendly.

She wasn't sure how to answer him, her only acquaintance with policemen being that of waving to one occasionally as she crossed a street somewhere in downtown Reno, or saying good morning to one she chanced to meet. She shook her head, but suddenly imagined her wild black hair, its thickness hanging loosely to frame flushed red cheeks. Red was her favorite color for Christmas decorations; heck, red was her favorite color no matter where it was. She giggled.

The policeman's gray eyes were suddenly menacing as he watched her. He reached into his jacket pocket and removed a pad and pen. "May I see your license, please?"

Concentrating with an effort, she slid her hand around on the car seat, searching for her handbag. Her hands were shaking as she removed her license and handed it to him. He continued to look at her, not at the license he held.

"I think we'll take you by the station for a breath test. Will you submit to that?"

"I'm not drunk," she said, hiccuping over her giggles. "I'm on my way to work at Conan Enterprises, over there." She gave a vague wave of her hand in the general direction of the big office complex that housed the engineering business.

His look became threatening. "We can't force you to take the test, of course," he said, and she got the impression he wanted to add, "but you'd better, or else." He got out of the car and walked around the back to her side. "Step outside, please."

He held the door as she got out and stood near him, swaying. Big white flakes of snow were covering his dark blue policeman's hat and the jacket that stretched over wide shoulders. She was dimly aware of the patrol car with red lights flashing as it pulled up behind them.

"Is this your current address, Miss?" the policeman asked, pen now poised over a book of tickets.

I'm not Miss. I'm Mrs., she wanted to tell him; at least for a few more weeks, that is.

She didn't move or answer him, and he finally raised his eyes from the pad, his mouth a straight line and his eyes dark with controlled anger. His gaze went from tumbled hair filled with snow to her wide eyes sparkling at him. She returned the look. *He's been taking lessons from Ken and is convinced I can't do anything right,* she decided. Ken was the one that put the Mrs. in her name, the one that soon would be removed.

"Ma'am?" The ice in that one word, coupled with the wind blowing snow over them, slid through her body, starting a shivering she couldn't control.

He's handsome, she thought, *but he shouldn't frown like that; it causes wrinkles.* That's what the house mother at the orphanage where she was raised used to tell all the children. "Smile, it's easier and looks better" was what they'd been taught. She pulled her tight face muscles into what she thought was a smile, but the man in front of her didn't return it.

Instead, his face slowly distorted, blending with the snow, and the next thing she knew, she was looking up at him from the pavement. A sharp pain lanced through her side, and she drew in a sharp breath, biting into her lower lip. The flashing lights on the patrol car behind them sent flickering red-and-white shadows over the policeman's face, giving him a ghostly appearance.

Everything took on a dreamlike quality; perhaps she was dreaming. Her voice almost inaudible, she said, "My boss's name is Conan. His number is..." Her voice trailed away as the effort to talk became too much, and she stopped, staring up at him with unblinking eyes.

For a big man Sergeant Mike Gresham moved swiftly as he stooped beside Joy, calling out to someone behind him. He lifted her head from the pavement. "Tell me your name."

Tiredness spread through her, and all she wanted to do was go to sleep. Stretching her eyes wide open, she managed a smile. "Joy." Joy to the world. Ken thought her name was flashy, along with all her other faults. But Ken's opinion no longer mattered. She started to apologize to the policeman for such a pretentious name at this time of year but decided it didn't matter.

Sighing, she went limp, and his arms tightened

around her. It was a good feeling to have strong, warm arms supporting her. He smelled masculine and clean, the wool of his uniform jacket rough on her cheek.

The man he'd called stood beside him, a shadow behind her half-closed eyes. They talked in subdued tones, both of them kneeling on the pavement. A blanket covered her, and she was carried to the backseat of the car, then held tightly to the chest of one of the men.

The door closed, and a moment later, another door slammed and the car moved. The siren started, and she opened her eyes to look straight into the policeman's gray ones, no longer cold and angry but dark and worried.

"Joy?" Funny, when he said it, the name didn't sound flashy or pretentious.

She burrowed her face into his chest and listened to the wail of the siren. It stopped simultaneously with the movement of the car, and she was lifted again, placed on a stretcher, and became a part of bustling activity.

"Joy?"

She turned her head. Ken sat by her bed. His eyes seemed dark with worry and...what else? Chagrin? Ken was her husband; all right, ex-husband. Knowing him well, she could imagine how he felt when Dr. Ross told him she'd lost their baby. Ken hadn't known Joy was pregnant; neither had she.

Perhaps she should have suspected, but the calendar had never coincided with her body's functions, and over the years, she'd come to ignore her irregularities. Not so Ken; he expected everything to happen on schedule. "Don't forget to take your pill, Joy." "Must you wear that tight sweater? Or that purple one?" "Do something with that hair." And a miscarriage with *his* child was simply unacceptable.

"Hello, Ken," she said now.

"Why didn't you tell me you were pregnant, Joy?" Anger came into the indulgent tone of his voice. "You can come back home now where you belong." Why hadn't she noticed his smugness before? Too much in love, naturally.

Back home was the house Ken had shared with Sharon, his first wife, who had died after a long illness, and Penny, their quiet, beautiful seven-year-old daughter. After two years of marriage Joy finally conceded and gave in to Sharon's ghost. Two months ago she moved from the house into a small serviceable apartment nearer her office. She hadn't moved soon enough, evidently.

"I didn't know I was pregnant," she told him now, watching him with a sort of detached curiosity.

He smiled, gently rubbing his fingers back and forth across the hand he was holding. "No wonder you've been so irritable and out of sorts."

She had always been the one out of focus, never Ken. He still believed her moving out of his house a couple of months earlier had been a childish display of bad temper and that she'd return as soon as she was finished pouting. She had no intention of going back.

When she married Ken, it was forever, and even she had no idea forever was so brief. But she couldn't go back and play second fiddle to a ghost.

Ken stood up. "Dr. Ross wants you to stay in the hospital several days, Joy, because of an infection. Do you want me to bring some of your nightgowns for you?"

"No, thank you." The hospital gowns would be fine for the brief time she was to be there, and it didn't bother her that they weren't satin and lace. Another one of Ken's many sore spots that she irritated during their short marriage.

Her hand slid down the front of the rough material of the hospital gown, and she thought of the chest of drawers still in Ken's bedroom. It held the lovely nightgowns he'd bought on special occasions, still wrapped in scented tissue. She preferred to sleep in jerseys with slogans in faded print, or football numbers, or pictures of dogs and kittens. They were comfortable, and if she ripped one in her rush to get things done around the house, she didn't have to worry about how much it had cost. The times Ken made love to her she wanted nothing between them, and it didn't seem right somehow to leave the filmy garments in a heap on the floor.

Ken left her with the assurance he'd be back the next day. He'd been notified she was in the hospital because he was still listed as her next of kin on the insurance card in her billfold. When she figured out whom to put in his place, she'd remove his name. She didn't need or want his concern anymore.

But Ken was faithful, coming by the hospital for the next two days, telling her she must come home with him to be looked after as soon as she was released. She wasn't going back there with him; for two years she'd tried to win what she thought was her rightful place with Ken, but Sharon was always between them, a lovely ghost he refused to let rest.

The final realization that she ran a slow third behind his first wife and his child forced her to make a decision. And she had; she left him with Sharon and Penny. If she still had a hangover of feelings for Ken, she'd lose it eventually. The miscarriage would make no difference.

As Joy stood at the window watching the new snow fall, a knock on the door interrupted her rebellious thoughts. When the door opened she stared at the policeman who had accused her of being drunk. *Now comes the request for my presence in court,* she thought. *The snow doesn't stop them from doing their duty.*

"Mrs. Strayer?"

"Yes." She liked the way he'd said "Joy" better.

He hesitated. "May I come in?"

She nodded and indicated the straight chair nearby as she went to sit on the bed.

"I'm Mike Gresham, and I came to apologize," he said, still standing by the door.

"It's all right. I understand." She couldn't fault him for doing his job, and he couldn't be expected to read minds, nor was he a doctor to recognize the fact that she had been ill.

He cleared his throat. "Alcohol frequently causes

flushed cheeks and brightness in the eyes, and you certainly had those symptoms." He smiled nervously.

"I said it's all right," she told him and shrugged. "Maybe the judge will be lenient and not take any points off my license."

"You didn't get a traffic ticket. It just took a while for me to realize you were sick instead of intoxicated."

"Oh," she said, and smiled for the first time. "Good. I've never had a traffic ticket, and I wasn't looking forward to it right here at Christmas." She pushed at the heavy hair brushing her cheek, suddenly wondering what she looked like. She'd barely looked in the mirror as she combed the dark mass of hair, not really caring how it looked or which way it fell.

"How long will you be here?" Mike asked.

"Till Friday, probably," she said, smiling a little. "They try to get rid of goldbrickers before the weekend."

He frowned. "Will you be all right by then?"

"Yes, I'm very healthy." The morning she'd met Mike was the only day she'd felt bad, and she had no time to realize there was anything wrong until she fainted there on the street. She couldn't remember any sicknesses other than colds, nothing that caused her to miss school or work.

His gaze went over her from her head to the bare feet hanging over the edge of the bed, bright red toenails a startling contrast to her white skin. Self-conscious, she drew her feet up under the frayed edge of the hospital robe.

He grinned. "Those aren't the most glamorous garments in the world, are they?" His eyes turned sober. "I'm very sorry about your losing the baby. Do you have children?"

"No." She kept her voice carefully even. There was no way Mike could know she didn't have a husband, either, anymore. She was just beginning to realize it herself.

He nodded and turned to leave. "Take care of yourself."

His brief visit made her feel better after all the brooding over the circumstances. It had taken a long time, but she was convinced she'd done the right thing by leaving Ken. The plain and simple truth was that she was not what he needed, and she wanted something more for herself, someone of her own who'd love her, faults and all, without comparing her to another.

A basket of bronze and white mums arrived later that day with a card that said: "Love, Ken and Penny." Quiet, respectable, solemn mums. They belonged to someone else—she would never fit that description. An unaccustomed sadness sent her to bed to bury her face in the pillow.

Early the next morning, Joy put on a clean hospital gown and walked around the big, sparse room. Her eyes rested on the basket of mums from Ken, and tied around the bottom of the basket was, of all things, a bright red ribbon. She removed it, caught her hair up in a thick cluster and tied the ribbon around it. The mirror in the bathroom reflected lackluster blue eyes with tinted circles almost the same color beneath them. The bright ribbon relieved her paleness a little and boosted her sagging spirits.

There was a light knock on the open door, and she came out of the bathroom to see Sergeant Gresham. In his hand was a small basket of pansies, a riot of color against his dark blue uniform.

"Good morning," he said. "They roust you out early, don't they?"

"Oh, I was up long before they came around. Bunch of sleepyheads."

He offered the flowers to her and she took them, holding the small basket close to her, seeing the tiny white plush kitten nestled in the center of the flowers. Its eyes were bright blue.

"I was trying to say how sorry I am for being so rough on you. People who drive while under the influence of alcohol or drugs are a horrible menace, because it's usually the innocent ones they hurt." When she didn't speak, he went on, "You'd be shocked at how many of them are your age and younger."

"At nine o'clock in the morning?" she asked, wondering just how old he thought she was and not bothering to enlighten him.

"Even at six in the morning," he said.

She looked down at the colorful flowers she held. "You didn't need to do this."

He smiled. "I know. I was on my way home from night shift and a friend fixed them for me."

"An all-night florist?" she teased.

"Well," he said, and laughed. "He owes me a couple of favors."

"They're the most cheerful spot in the hospital," she said. Yellow, red and purple faces peeked at her from the basket.

"Still think you'll be out by Friday?"

"Yes. Dr. Ross came by to see me last night and promised to release me by then."

"I'm glad." He turned to the door. His eyes went from the red ribbon holding her hair, down the shapeless gown to her bare feet. "Take care of yourself and have a Merry Christmas."

Merry Christmas. Joy loved the bright decorations of the season, loved the hustle and bustle, the crush of the crowds, the last-minute scurrying for presents and the Christmas carols. Ken didn't; there wasn't so much as a wreath on their door; no baking, no... Resolutely, she turned her back on her life with Ken and thought ahead about the few weeks before Christmas this year. She'd refused Ken's demand—he never asked—that she come "home" to recuperate.

On Friday, she took a cab to her apartment, then called the office as soon as she sat down. Tom Conan, her boss, was back from his trip to Chicago, and she smiled as he groused about her waiting till he left town to get sick.

"Take off as much time as you need, honey," he told her. "Don't come back here too soon. That's an order."

Two hours later, a dozen red roses were delivered from him.

Tom Conan, founder and owner of Conan Enterprises, a highly respected engineering firm, was her
first real love. Sent by her high school Distributive
Education teacher to the First National Bank for an
interview, she didn't get the job, but in the bank's
computer room she was fascinated by the machines,
asking question after question about their program-
ming and functions. Joy was an average student in
everything except her math courses. In all of them,
from basic math through calculus, she carried straight
A's all the way through school. She fell in love with
the complicated studies as soon as she found out she
could manipulate numbers to do anything she wanted
them to do.

One of the supervisors in the computer room
stopped to talk to her, and when she displayed some
knowledge of the computer concepts, he said, "I have
a friend who might give you a job. You could go talk
to him."

The friend was Tom Conan. She had gone to Conan
Enterprises, a green high school senior with only curiosity and a zest for life going for her.

As Tom Conan looked over her high school credits,
he frowned, and she swallowed over the disappointment she was already feeling at not getting this job.
She had come with such high hopes and watched with
misgivings as he went over her papers before looking
up to meet her worried eyes.

"What makes you think you'd like to work for Conan Enterprises, Joy?" he asked.

She stared at him, the narrow thin face with

hawkishly straight nose, blue eyes regarding her steadily.

"Mr. Long at First National said he's a friend of yours, and you might hire me because I like numbers."

He didn't smile. "There's more to a job at Conan's than numbers, young lady."

She bit her lip and suddenly saw a room with numbers chasing one another around and smiled at the ridiculous sight, her dimples appearing and disappearing again. She drew in her breath.

"I'm not a real whiz in school, but math is my best subject, probably because I can remember figures quite well and can relate them to any given subject," she explained. "Mr. Long said...that is, he thought..."

Tom Conan waited as she floundered, searching for the words she wanted. When she looked up from her tightly clasped fingers after a long silence, he smiled at her.

"If Ace Long says you're all right, I won't argue."

She straightened to look questioningly at him as he consulted her application once more. "We'll need to know your next of kin and family background, Joy."

"I'm hired?"

"You're hired, Joy. Now report to Personnel and fill out insurance and beneficiary forms. You start work Monday."

She sat still until he raised his brows, looking at her over the edge of the papers. "I don't have any family, Mr. Conan," she said slowly. "My parents were killed when I was two years old, and I've been at the Greenbriar Orphanage since then."

He continued to look at her, and she wondered if not having a family meant she wouldn't get the job. Joy envied classmates who fought with brothers and sisters, and she hated her status of never really belonging to anyone. She was going to hate it even more if it kept her from getting this job she wanted so badly.

The stern-looking man cleared his throat. "Report to Personnel, Joy. If you want to make the orphanage your beneficiary, it can be arranged."

Tom had given Joy the first—and only—job she'd ever held, watched her struggle through college and, when she reached age twenty-three, gave her a technical assistant's job that consisted of a lot of long, tedious research: columns of figures that had to match everything else in the firm's estimates.

Two years later she was promoted to head his marketing division, going all over the country with her own plans and manuals to talk to everyone from big bosses to ditchdiggers. At the ripe old age of twenty-eight, she watched her pay raises come regularly as she went on learning from clients she met every day and from the professionals at Conan's, not the least of which was the boss himself. Tom never had reason to regret hiring the teenager many years ago, and she'd loved him from day one, a tall gray-haired gentleman with an iron-tough exterior and a heart of pure gold.

IT WAS THE DAY before Christmas Eve when Joy drove her car for the first time since the miscarriage. Ready to climb the walls from boredom, told by the doctor to not even so much as vacuum, she dressed warmly before going to the mall to see the Christmas decorations.

The city decorated the courtyard inside the mall each year, and she loved the intricately working toys, trains and dolls in the windows as much as any of the small children. Parking on a side street, she walked through the open area, listening to the sounds of Christmas. A Salvation Army captain stood by his black kettle, ringing the tinny-sounding bell. Children gathered around a Santa Claus who shouted, "Merry Christmas! Ho! Ho! Ho!" and she smiled at him.

Snow was beginning to fall again, and she was glad she had on the lavender all-weather coat with the warm zip-out lining—the one Ken thought garish-looking. It had been on sale, an expensive coat Joy liked instantly, proud of its being so pretty and available for such a good price. It hadn't impressed Ken at all; face it, nothing she did impressed him.

Her hands were stuck in her pockets because she could never find two matching gloves. The black boots she wore had been a Christmas present from Ken the year before.

Joy was bareheaded, and her hair was soon covered by big snowflakes as she walked across the small footbridge away from the huge tree and turned to look back at it. It was beautiful: bright and glowing with color, the way Christmas should be, and she stood taking it all in.

"I may still take you in for a breathalyzer test," a teasing voice said behind her. "Anyone out in this weather when she doesn't have to be must be under the influence of something."

Chapter Two

A curious thrill went through her as she swung around to face the man in civilian clothing standing a few feet away from her.

"Hello, Sergeant Gresham. Merry Christmas."

He smiled down at her and nodded toward the tree. "Are you alone?"

"Yes." She let her gaze go over him, his bare head showing plenty of silvery gray alongside the white flakes of snow that caught in his thick hair. She had forgotten how big he was, so tall that her head was tilted way back to look up at him.

"How have you been doing?" he asked, his eyes searching hers, going over her face as if to refresh his memory.

She shrugged. "I'm okay."

He hesitated a moment before he said, "I'm off duty. How about a cup of coffee?"

"All right." She gave a quick acceptance because even the small amount of walking she'd done had tired her.

They strolled down the street to a small coffee shop, and as they were seated, he asked, "Did you have lunch?"

A glance at her watch showed it was almost two o'clock. She shook her head. "I'm not hungry, but I'd really prefer hot chocolate to coffee."

"Hot chocolate it is." He gave the order to the waitress, whom he evidently knew well. Then again policemen always knew people who ran coffee shops, their mainstay in any weather.

She looked up to find his eyes openly surveying her.

"You need to gain some weight," he said.

"I'm saving up so I can eat all the holiday goodies."

"Do you bake a lot during the Christmas season?"

"Not this year. I haven't done a thing." Nor last year, either, she could have added. Ken didn't believe in making such a mess in the kitchen when you could buy whatever you wanted in the stores. At that moment, she realized she missed Penny more than she did Ken—she could at least satisfy the little girl by baking the brownies she loved.

Her expression must have told him more than her words. He opened his mouth as though to say something else but continued to just look at her until the waitress returned with two hot chocolates.

"How about some of Maude's cookies with that, Mike?" the girl asked.

"That sounds good, Paula."

"Who's Maude?" Joy asked as the girl turned away.

"Paula's sister. They own the coffee shop, and

Maude supplies the neighborhood with her special cookies at Christmas every year.''

Paula returned with a heaping plate of rumball and pecan cookies, and Joy smiled at her as she placed them in the center of the table.

"This is Joy Strayer, Paula. I almost arrested her for driving while intoxicated, and I'm trying to get out of the doghouse.''

Paula looked at Joy and turned incredulous eyes to Mike. "Her? DWI? Mike, you're losing your touch.''

He looked crestfallen. "I guess so.'' They laughed, and Joy wondered at the joke.

Paula saw her questioning expression and explained. "Mike sniffs out DWIs like a bloodhound, and most of his arrests result in convictions. But you, Joy.'' She shook her head. "Mike, how could you?''

Mike grinned across at Joy, his eyes holding an odd look. "She had bright sparkling eyes and red cheeks, and she giggled. I thought she was Mrs. Claus, celebrating early.'' Paula laughed and moved away to her other customers.

Concentrating on the cookies and hot chocolate, Joy looked up to meet Mike's gaze and blushed. Probably in an unconsciously juvenile defiance of Ken's criticism of the way she dressed, she was wearing a white knit turtleneck sweater that hugged her down to the hips, which were plainly outlined in white corduroy jeans. Even with her recent weight loss, there was no room for another wrinkle if she'd had one. A small reindeer Penny had given her was pinned at the beginning curve of her left breast.

Mike's eyes rested on the reindeer a moment and returned to her face. He said, unexpectedly, "I'd like to take you home to meet my mother, Joy." He laughed softly to let her know it was a kidding remark.

Keeping her voice light, she asked, "Where does Mrs. Gresham live?"

"Denver."

She swallowed a mouthful of hot chocolate, burning her tongue, and stared at him. Denver was a thousand miles away.

He straightened up and looked at his own cup. "Forget I said that."

She remembered then that he didn't know she no longer had a husband—or soon wouldn't have. She smiled to let him know she understood he was kidding and said, "I'd better finish my shopping and get on home. Thanks for the drink."

Leaving Mike at the door of the shop, Joy walked through the department store nearest her, stopping by a counter to stare unseeing at the merchandise there. She had no Christmas shopping to do, no presents to buy for anyone. She sent her usual check to Greenbriar Orphanage, and Tom dared anyone to buy him presents, even though he was generous to his employees. He was all the family she had left, but one thing she didn't have to worry about—Tom approved of almost everything she did.

Moving past the crowds of holiday shoppers, Joy lifted her head and squared her shoulders. There was a new year on the way, and she had lots of living to do. No one says you can't do it alone, she thought.

But all she'd ever wanted to do was share all the love within her saved over the years. Joy was good at sharing. Brought up at Greenbriar Orphanage, she wore hand-me-downs that came to her if there was any use left in them. Her hurried ways were left over from the time when she'd had too many things to do and not enough hours in the day to do them. There was always a bump to kiss, a diaper to change, a pair of dirty little hands to wash, someone needing just a hug and sympathetic shoulder to lean on for a much-needed boost.

As she grew up, too old to be adopted and too young to be turned loose on her own, she watched the other girls grow streamlined figures with high, tight breasts, while she held on to the baby fat the house-mothers were so fond of calling her soft chubbiness. She had all the enemies of a teenage girl, including pimples on her chin. Her hair, jet black, stuck in tight corkscrew curls against her head. And no matter how often she dieted and stayed away from her beloved strawberry milkshakes, the hated baby fat refused to go away.

As the years slid past, she didn't notice her skin clearing to become creamy smooth, twin dimples flashing at her quick smile, or her corkscrew curls turning into deep, shining waves that she brushed carelessly back to lie on her shoulders. In her rush to see what life had to offer, she missed the changes in her body from baby fat to curves distributed with a gentle hand over her five feet, three inches of height. The eyes, so far apart there was room for two of the turned up buttons she called a nose, became wide-set and black-lashed, the color of dew-wet wood violets. Orphanages can't afford orthodontists, and though her teeth were healthy and white, one front tooth rested slightly over another one, and she developed a habit of covering it with the tip of her tongue.

"May I help you, ma'am?"

Joy looked up to see a woman nearby and realized she had stopped at a counter of lingerie. She hadn't seen any of the delicate lacy items; her thoughts had been far away from the milling crowds. Shaking her head at the question, she walked on through a side door and back to her car.

CHRISTMAS AND NEW YEAR'S WENT the way of all holidays, and Joy was glad to get back to work, filling her mind with facts and figures that, for a while each day, kept her thoughts away from anything personal. It was becoming easier to live with the idea of being a divorcée, something she'd never associated with herself.

She filled nonworking hours with indoor tennis, reading everything she could find, even horseback riding through the parks, quiet now with the cold weather except for occasional hardy joggers.

Tom came to her one morning, dropping his tall, still-straight body into the chair near her desk. "We're going to reopen the Red Lodge project, Joy. I hope you didn't throw all that stuff away." His white eyebrows lifted as he grinned at her. He knew she never threw anything of her project material away.

She sat up straight. The dam project in Red Lodge, Montana, a tiny town perched on the banks of a swiftly flowing stream, had been one of her favorites. Three years earlier Tom gave her the task of working out the marketing and insurance programs. Her research had taken her into the near wilderness of the towering mountains, tracing the course of the river, studying the effects the dam would have on Red Lodge and the surrounding natural environs.

Her files grew as she traveled back and forth, gathering material to feed into the complex system of computers to come up with the program to fit the engineering phase of building the dam that had been proposed by city, county, state and federal agencies. Everything came to a halt when environmentalists won an injunction against Conan Enterprises. The dam was badly needed to supply power and could be built well within environmental standards.

And that, too, had been a source of irritation to Ken. After Joy married Ken, she still had work to do on the marketing portion of the program: meeting with the townspeople and town council in Red Lodge, estimating the number of local employees, skilled and unskilled, they would need; running the factors through the computers to give a ballpark figure of dollars that would filter into the economy of the small town. Joy was gone overnight several times until Ken put his foot down, and Tom gave the files over to Will Baker for him to follow up.

"We can go ahead with it?" she asked now, her cheeks flushing with interest.

"Yes. The injunction has been modified enough that we can work with it. However, you'll need to revamp your program completely." He watched her now. "How long will that take you?"

"Working some overtime, give me a month."

"Look, Joy. Whatever you do, take care of yourself. We've waited this long, a couple of more weeks won't hurt," Tom told her.

"I'll be careful," she promised.

Still he watched her. "No chance of reconciliation between you and Ken?"

"None." She gave him a direct look, and Tom knew she didn't want to talk about the upcoming divorce. It was still a sore spot, although the hurt was receding, but her feeling of helpless frustration still erupted sometimes.

I don't know, she was thinking now as she pulled files from the drawers to choose the ones she'd take home to work on. *Maybe everybody who gets divorced asks "Why me?" and wonders where things got completely out of hand.* It hadn't worked out for them, and that was sad, but it wasn't the end of the world.

Slamming the drawers shut, she stacked folders on the desk, then carried them out to her car. At home, she reversed the process, placing the folders on the floor by the table where she could reach them.

She was engrossed in the maps Cliff Decker, chief engineer consultant at Conan's, had drawn up for her. How much of the original dam area would they be able to keep? That would determine how many thousand cubic feet of water they would maintain at high level without danger of flooding Red Lodge and the surrounding area. There was very little adjusting she could do until she took another look at the site.

The phone rang and she automatically glanced at the clock on the kitchen wall. Nine o'clock. Where had the time gone? She grinned to herself. When she became immersed in figures, she forgot everything.

"Hello?" Her pencil was poised over a figure that looked high, and she bent to see if she had transposed a five to an eight.

"Joy?"

The pencil dropped onto the figures, which blurred in front of her as she heard Ken's voice. She stiffened.

"Yes, Ken. How are you?"

"More to the point, how are you?" His deep voice was soft with concern. "I dropped by Dr. Ross's office today, and he said you'd been in for your checkup."

"I'm doing quite well, thank you." Well, if you know I'm all right, what's your problem, she wanted to ask.

"Joy." She wasn't accustomed to having Ken hesitate when talking to her, and he had her attention. "Well, that's all I need to know, that you're doing okay alone." He waited, but she didn't say anything. The idea that Joy could exist without him was unthinkable. Same old Ken. No self-doubt, but plenty of doubt about Joy.

A few more pleasantries as she asked about Penny, and then Ken hung up. She waited, but she felt no immediate depression the way it had once been, no hurting in her chest. All that was left was the tiny pang of regret for something she'd thought was forever.

Shrugging away the interruption, Joy went back to her figures. She *had* mistaken an eight; maybe she needed glasses.

THE SECOND WEEK IN APRIL, Joy and Tom flew to Billings, Montana, and rented a car to drive to the proposed dam site a few miles from Red Lodge. It was cold in Montana, even though weather at home in Reno was pleasant and mild in the early spring.

"Dress warm, Joy. The wind coming off the mountains is icy," Tom warned.

She wore gray knit pants and a heavy sweater, boots and a red jacket insulated against the cold but lightweight. She brought the hood up over her hair, drawing the string tight. They walked alongside the stream to the spot where boulders had been placed a year ago to mark the beginning of the area to be taken in by the dam facility.

Tom stood with his hands in his overcoat pockets, bareheaded, the wind teasing his white hair until it stood in peaks. "I don't really blame the people for not wanting the dam, Joy. It's almost sacrilege to destroy this quietness."

She nodded, but they both knew more power was needed, not only in Red Lodge, but eventually in other nearby rural areas.

That evening they had dinner with the town council, deciding on a go-ahead date for the work to begin.

"How long will the actual construction take, Mr. Conan?" Carl Monks, the chairman, asked.

Joy handed the sheet of figures to Tom showing her projection of the time involved and the employment requirements. He studied the page and looked around him.

"Two and a half to three years," he said. "It will bring added employment to Red Lodge as well as to Billings. The more skilled and semiskilled laborers we can hire locally, the better off our company will be."

A general murmur of approval went around the room. The meeting broke up on an optimistic note, and they went back to the motel in good spirits.

"Barring several natural disasters and a complete breakdown of equipment, we'll have a completely safe dam, more than an adequate supply of water for the sheds, and power to burn, so to speak," Tom said, rubbing his hands together in satisfaction. "And still leave the land in good shape."

"You love this stuff, don't you?" she asked. "Most bosses at your age would let someone younger come out on jobs such as this one, to freeze to death and walk your legs off."

"At my age?" He turned his eyes away from the road to look at her. "Just because you're still a teenager doesn't mean I'm over the hill, Joy."

"Teenager? Boy, are you behind the times."

He was watching the road again. "You still seem seventeen to me, Joy." He shook his head. "That day you came to see me, I thought, now, you know, there's nobody as young as this girl is. Then you flashed your dimples at me."

"What did the dimples have to do with it?" she asked as he let the silence settle between them.

He laughed. "I decided to hire you anyway, dimples or not, still wet behind the ears or not. I was afraid the next place you applied for a job might not be trustworthy and might not take care of you."

Ken didn't think she could take care of herself; Tom didn't, either. She faced the thin asphalt ribbon of road ahead of them and thought philosophically, *Well, I'll show them. At twenty-eight, I should be able to make it on my own.* But her glance at Tom was affectionate. He was a wonderful boss and a wonderful man.

Chapter Three

Giving the courts a restless going over, Mike Gresham did a double take when he saw the small figure several yards away from him. Joy Strayer—the case of mistaken identity as a DWI offender. The lonely wanderer around Santa Claus and the Christmas shoppers. The hot-chocolate drinker.

She was seated on a bench apparently concentrating on the tennis raquet she tapped against the toe of her sneakers. His gaze sought nearby people, looking for her husband or someone else who might be a tennis partner. She paid no attention to anyone on the courts, nor did anyone seem aware of her.

Suddenly he remembered the feeling he'd had when he picked her up from the sidewalk after she fainted. A sort of "watch it, Mike" voice had sounded within him. He'd marked it off as just being careful he didn't cause the city to be hit with a civil suit for being rough with her when she was sick. After his casual mention of taking her home to his mother, he'd decided he must be out of his mind even to think lightly about a married woman.

Only a couple of times since then had he thought
about her. Once when he'd seen a small woman crossing North Virginia Avenue, jet black hair blowing
across a small face. It wasn't Joy Strayer, and he'd
shrugged his shoulders, impatiently wondering what
was the matter with him.

He was a senior sergeant in the Reno police force,
and he knew what illicit relations with a married woman
could do to him. He'd seen careers thrown away for
that very reason. Not Mike Gresham. He was a career
man, and a career in his chosen field left little room for
a woman. Unless that woman was as strong as Goliath,
broadminded as hell and had as much interest in his job
and sympathy for the human race as he had.

So for four months he had forgotten about Joy
Strayer.

"Hello, Joy."

He knew it was a mistake the moment she raised
her head and her blue eyes met his. For a moment,
there was no recognition there; then the blank look
disappeared and she smiled. And Sergeant Mike
Gresham caught his breath.

Twin dimples appeared in the faintly flushed cheeks
as she smiled up at him, the tip of her tongue darting
out to touch the white tooth that was slightly out of line.
It was the sexiest move he'd ever seen, and he was sure
she was unaware of it.

"Hello, Mike."

He sat down beside her and surveyed the couples
on the courts. "Your husband out there?"

She shook her head, letting her gaze go over the
players.

He waited, and when she said nothing, he asked, "Do you need a partner?" He took in her white terry shirt and brief navy tennis shorts.

"Yes."

"Will you take me?" he asked, aware of the double entendre of the question, grinning as he said it.

"Okay." If she noticed any double meaning to his question, she ignored it.

They played two sets. He won the first and she won the second. "I must be getting old and out of shape," he said. "I've never let a little twerp like you beat me before."

"You may be right," she agreed pleasantly.

"About what?"

"You're old and out of shape."

"Hey, I was only kidding," he protested. She smiled at him, a sweet smile for an old friend.

"Do you have to go home immediately?" he asked on the way to the dressing area. *Watch it, Mike; this could get antsy.* He squashed the warning voice and waited for her answer. To his surprise, he was anxious to hear a negative reply.

"No."

He stopped and looked down at her. "How about a soda at Paula's?"

"All right."

"Meet you outside in fifteen minutes," he said.

Joy watched Mike walk away from her, noticing for the first time his slim hips in white shorts and his long muscular legs.

Earlier, her hair had been bound with a piece of white yarn and now she had brushed it out, letting it swing loose to her shoulders. She had put on a yellow cotton shirt with yellow checked pants and had slipped barefoot into sandals, throwing her things into an old navy tote bag. Mike was waiting as she ran down the outside steps.

"Looks like you forgot to eat all the Christmas goodies," he said, eyeing her too-slender figure.

She slanted a look at him. "When I get to be your age, I'll have to watch my weight."

"That's unfair," he said as they fell into step.

"Truth usually is," she said.

"Are you picking on me, Joy?"

"Sorry," she said, concentrating on missing the cracks in the sidewalk. It had been one of her bad days, when self-doubt reared its ugly head. Doubt that she'd ever forget her two years of married life with Ken; doubt that she'd ever get over the feeling that the failure of the marriage was entirely her fault.

Not only that, but all the figures she'd put together on the marketing program for the dam in Red Lodge were so far off, she'd had to start over. With inflation eating away at the economy and hourly wages almost twice what they'd been when Conan's bid was submitted, her previous figures were ridiculous. Tom, aware of the problem, reassured her they had plenty of time. But patience wasn't one of Joy's strong points.

Mike said nothing more as they turned into the small coffee shop.

Paula stopped when she saw them. "Joy," she said, "has he arrested you again?"

"No, but he did promise me a soda after I beat him at tennis."

"You deserve it if you beat Mike. He's death on the tennis court. What kind of soda would you like?" she asked.

"Strawberry."

"Me, too," Mike said, and waited as Joy slid into the booth before he sat down opposite her. He was quiet until she looked up to meet his gaze. "Got problems, Joy?"

She shrugged. "Doesn't everyone?"

"Anything I can do?"

Joy eyed the man across from her. He was old enough to be married, probably in his mid-thirties, but he wore no ring. Of course, people got divorced; look at Joy Strayer, also old enough to be married. She didn't wear a ring, either. Self-consciously she glanced at the third finger of her left hand, clasped loosely with her right. The light line left by her rings was still visible. She dropped her hands into her lap.

But Mike noticed her attempt to hide her past, and his eyes followed her hands, then swung back to meet hers.

She answered the question he was too polite to ask. "Ken and I are separated." She bit into her lip, then raised her chin a little. "Divorce pending."

"Is that what's bothering you?"

"It doesn't bother me anymore."

"Looks like Joy tells lies," he said gently.

Paula chose that moment to bring their sodas, and for a moment Joy didn't reply to that statement.

When she sat back in the booth and faced him, he was smiling.

"I guess you're right, Mike, but mostly she lies to Joy." Her tone was rueful, and after a bit, she went on, correcting herself. "*Most* of the time, it doesn't bother me. It's just that sometimes, it seems there should have been something we could have done." Her shoulders lifted in a restless move, and she went back to sipping her strawberry drink.

"Everyone feels the same way," he said quietly, watching her as she watched the straw in the glass.

She looked up. "Everyone?"

He grinned. "I don't speak from personal experience, just as an observer."

"Sergeant Gresham, the saver of helpless souls; Sergeant Gresham, the philosopher."

"I get extra pay for that service." He laughed across the table at her.

"Thanks for the uplifting conversation."

"Anytime, Joy." He was still smiling. "My mother would still like to meet you."

The tension inside her eased a bit at his teasing comment. Knowledge that Mike thought her attractive gave her sagging morale a much-needed boost.

"Where do you live?" Mike asked.

"The LaCrosse Circle apartments."

"The new ones on the south side?"

"Yes."

He studied her face, the full lips parted as she licked the ice cream from them, the dark blue eyes that shaded to violet. "Let's go to my place, and I'll fix us a steak." Joy looked up at him, and he grinned. "I'm a good cook. How about it?"

There was no need for her to hurry back to the apartment. "All right. I'll follow you in my car."

Mike's place was a townhouse across the city in the fashionable northwest corner. It was beautiful, furnished in elegantly mixed period furniture. A huge living room went the full length of the other rooms with all glass in the front and a view over the city.

"I didn't know policemen made this kind of money," she said, taking in the simple luxury of the room.

He laughed. "It belongs to my mother."

She widened her eyes at him and said, "Maybe I should go meet the lady."

"Do that. But first come help me."

The steaks were perfect, and they shared cleanup duties without talking. As they finished, he said, "I also mix an excellent brandy Alexander."

She smiled. "You're in luck. I've never had one, so I have no means of comparison. However, being from Reno, I'm willing to gamble."

He brought the drinks and sat beside her on the couch. She sipped the frothy drink, tasting the spicy flavoring, swallowed and licked her lips, looking up at him. As Joy opened her mouth to speak, he leaned to kiss her, his mouth firm and cool from his drink. His hand tangled in her hair, pulling her head back, his eyes wide open looking into hers.

The stirrings inside her were warm and familiar, and she stared back into his eyes, surprised that she could feel response to an almost total stranger. But it had been a long time since she was held by a man, a long time since one had looked at her with that warmth in his eyes. For some reason, she recalled the worried dark eyes when he discovered she was sick instead of drunk, holding her close to his wide chest on the ride to the hospital.

"Your mouth is so kissable," he whispered. Their lips touched lightly again, and gradually the pressure increased, his hands moving to bring her body closer to him. He removed the drink from her hand, putting it on the table beside his, and, both hands free, pulled her to him.

It had been a long time since Joy was kissed, a long time without arms around her. The strength of his arms was tempered by the gentle way he held her, no roughness in his hands as they caressed her shoulders, moving down her back to the curve of her hips. She leaned into his body, lips parting beneath his demanding mouth, her hands gathering his shirt front as she clung to him.

Clinging hands spread on his chest, and she pushed him away, turning her head so she wouldn't have to look at him.

"Joy," he said softly.

"No, Mike, I'm married."

"But you're getting a divorce."

"Yes, but..." She shook her head as if to emphasize her reluctance to continue their lovemaking. He handed her the glass, and she took it, turning it round and round in her hands.

"Do you still love him?" he asked after a short silence.

"You can't just turn love off like a switch, Mike. It has to leave the way it grows—slowly." She stood up and walked across to the window, pushing the drapes aside to look out over the city of lemon-colored lights.

"Marriages aren't necessarily built to last longer than any other relationship, Joy. The sooner you realize that, the better off you'll be."

"You've never married, Mike?"

"No."

"You've never been in love?" Her gaze went over the face; rugged and intense; tanned skin stretched over high cheekbones; a thin, straight nose; and a mouth that was firm and sensuous at the same time. But his eyes were the real focal point; deep-set and gray, they could pin you to the wall with their piercing directness. She knew that from experience when he accused her of being drunk.

He smiled a little, meeting her quizzical look. "I never said that." Watching her, he went on. "A policeman's wife has to be someone special, Joy, with special abilities, foresight and insight, and tougher than her husband. I've never found anyone that tough." He stared at the glass in his hand instead of at her. "A policeman's wife is used as much as she's loved."

"Used?" She repeated the odd word.

"That's about it. She's used as a defense against everything he sees every day; all the hate, depression, cynicism, brute force." He was quiet a moment. "Love can only absorb so much of that before it turns on you and becomes vindictive in self-defense.'' He looked up. ''I've seen marriages that started out with love dissolve as though there had never been any feelings at all.'' He shook his head. ''It isn't fair to ask that of any woman, and that's why I've never married.''

She let the drapery drop from her hand and came back to stand in front of him. ''How sad—to be afraid to love because it might not last.''

His eyes narrowed. ''Aren't you afraid, Joy?''

She shook her head. ''Not even now, not of loving someone. Perhaps of that love not being returned. Love is necessary for me to exist.''

His voice picked up an angry inflection. ''Then you plan to keep on loving Ken?''

''Of course not, but...'' All those years in the orphanage, she'd had the younger children to love her, but no one she could really call her own. And her first venture into the land of romantic dreams of everlasting love was a mistake. The key word leaped out at her: *was*. She would have other chances. She pulled her shoulders up. ''You know, Mike, life is terribly unfair.''

''Yes, it is,'' he agreed. He stood up, smiling down at her. ''You need another drink.''

''No, I'd better go.'' Her watch said two o'clock, and wandering the streets in the early-morning hours had never appealed to her.

''Stay here tonight.'' Joy gave him a hard look, and he quickly explained, ''There are two bedrooms and you're welcome to one all to yourself.''

"No strings?"

"No strings," he assured her.

The thought of the lonely apartment was enough to decide for her. "All right, Mike," she said, and followed him across a short, wide hallway into a bedroom as large as her entire apartment. The walls were stark white with navy-blue drapes, spread and carpet. She could see a bathroom in the same colors through the open doorway.

"Wait," he said and disappeared into another room across the hall.

She had moved to stand near the bed when he returned with a pair of pajamas and a toothbrush.

He grinned. "A little better than the hospital gowns you wore the last time I saw you in bed." The grin faded. "It was a long time before I stopped thinking about you after we left you at the hospital that day. You were so little and crumpled-looking, and I was mad at myself for yelling at you." He held out the pajamas and toothbrush. "My partner that day was Jake Paraski, and he kept hoping Santa Claus would bring you to his house because he played the Good Samaritan."

"You can thank him for me."

"Come to headquarters sometime and I'll introduce you." He tilted her chin, placed his mouth on hers, and before she could react released her and moved to the door. "I go to work at six tomorrow, so you'll have to fix your own breakfast. Good night, Joy."

The pajama top swallowed her, but she slept wrapped

in the garment, which smelled clean and masculine, needing the warm, intimate feeling it gave her.

The apartment was empty when she woke, and a note propped on the kitchen counter said: "You're beautiful asleep—or otherwise. I'll never launder the pajama top again. Mike."

Joy picked up the note and slipped it into her handbag, not bothering to ask herself why. It was nine o'clock when she left the apartment without fixing any breakfast, and she drove across town in light Saturday-morning traffic. Ffiteen minutes later, she pulled into the parking space reserved for her at Conan Enterprises.

There was plenty of work for her to finish before she left for Red Lodge the following Wednesday morning.

Chapter Four

"What the hell, Joy?" It was Tom. "You've already put in sixty hours this week. I can't afford your overtime."

She blinked and rubbed the back of her neck, smiling up at him. "I expect to be a millionaire in ten years."

"A dead one," he grumbled. "It's nearly dinnertime. Let's go eat."

Shocked, she looked at her watch. She had worked straight through till five-thirty, and she hadn't had any breakfast. "You don't want to feed me," she said. "I haven't eaten since yesterday." Somehow, she wasn't hungry when she left Mike's that morning. She was emotionally full, if nothing else. The few minutes in Mike's arms left her with a feeling of uneasiness, and in that feeling she knew there lurked danger—either to her or to Mike.

Tom's face was a thundercloud. "Ken's right. You shouldn't be allowed to run loose."

Her head jerked upward. "When did he say that?"

Tom Conan was embarrassed, something she seldom saw. "He called me to ask how you were doing."

"What did you tell him?" Aside from one dutiful call after she returned to the apartment, she hadn't heard from him.

"The truth. You seem to be fine but were working too hard. He thinks you're not capable of taking care of yourself, and looking at you, I'm inclined to agree." His grumbling reminded her of what she supposed a worried father might sound like.

Silently, she gathered up her papers, put them in her briefcase, and locked them in her desk. If Tom hadn't been standing there, she'd have taken them home with her to work later or the following morning, but he'd have had a fit. She worked to cover the lonely hours when there was no one she could talk to or worry about. She chose never to worry about herself, and lately there seemed to be a lot of hours left over between sleep and work.

She looked up to find her boss watching her. "If you're buying, Godfather's Pizza is the best in town. Especially with a good red wine."

"Pizza? On Saturday night? You aren't looking out for my ulcer."

They walked down the hallway to the elevator, rode it down to the underground parking area where he kept his new Cadillac, and as he pulled out onto the street, she said, "Beautiful car." Tom Conan didn't waste money on new cars; he'd driven the last one ten years.

He grunted but didn't answer her, and she subsided quietly, not trying to make conversation. She was surprised when he stopped at Godfather's Pizza and turned to look at him.

"You said it was good," he reminded her.

It was a Saturday pizza crowd, lots of teenagers before the movies. It seemed longer than ten years since she was eighteen. She smiled across at Tom. *He must be thinking similar thoughts,* she thought.

They consumed a medium-sized pizza loaded with everything imaginable, plus a carafe of wine. She leaned back, wiped her mouth and yawned.

"The company, perhaps?" he asked.

"I got to bed very late and was up very early," she told him without giving out the secret of where she had spent the night. He definitely wouldn't understand such an uncharacteristic trait in his marketing consultant.

"Let's go, and you can catch up on your sleep. You're not to work at all tomorrow, do you understand?" His voice was quietly authoritative.

"Yes, sir," she said meekly.

He drove back to Conan's and stopped near her car. "Will you be all right getting home?"

"Contrary to what you and Ken may think, I believe I can find my way. Thanks for dinner. Good night, Tom." She slammed the door and went to unlock her own car. He waited until she pulled from the parking lot before he turned his car in the opposite direction. Her eyes burned with unshed tears as she drove the short distance to her apartment. She must be overtired, as Tom said; she'd just cut down on the extra work, as he suggested.

As she locked her car, the wailing of a siren sounded through the early-evening stillness. Mike Gresham's call to arms, his alarm to danger, the raucous blaring summons that made his life too dangerously demanding to share with just any woman. He didn't believe such a woman existed, one that could stand the rigors of his everyday life.

The echo of the siren died away in the distance, and she realized her attention had been riveted to the sound, wondering who was in trouble. She walked into her apartment and closed the door on the world outside.

SINCE SHE HAD PROMISED Tom she wouldn't work, Sunday threatened to be a long day. Joy dawdled over her coffee, then walked the six blocks to the newsstand to pick up a paper. She didn't subscribe to a daily, making use of the one available at the office, and she'd rather walk to pick up her Sunday paper than have it delivered.

The streets were comparatively empty of people or traffic; the silence was almost eerie. Even tourists slept late on Sundays before venturing out to eat, to take in the lounges they missed on Saturday night, or to visit more local attractions. Paper under her arm, she strolled leisurely back the way she had come, glancing into store windows, smiling at some of the ridiculous styles displayed on the fashionably skinny mannequins.

Back in her apartment, she put a couch cushion on the carpeted floor and spread the paper near her, lying for a moment staring at the ceiling. Sighing, she reached for the front section. "Well, world, what's happened to you since I last looked?" The headlines affirmed world unrest; the subheadings named countries and people familiar to those who paid any attention at all to what was going on around them. Local weather said clear with temperatures in the low seventies.

The picture in the bottom left-hand corner caught her eyes, and she looked into the smiling face of a police officer. Dark eyes looked straight into hers as he smiled, showing white teeth below a neatly trimmed mustache. Beneath the picture was the heading: POLICE OFFICER IN SERIOUS CONDITION. She continued reading. "Corporal Jake Paraski remained in serious but stable condition..."

Her heart stopped. Mike's partner. What about Mike? Frantically she read on "... condition at Wilshire General Hospital after being shot at close range by a man whom he and his partner had stopped for reckless driving about five o'clock Saturday afternoon. Sergeant Michael Gresham, the injured man's partner, escaped with minor injuries when the suspect shot Paraski in the shoulder and turned the gun on Gresham as he ran toward him from the patrol car. Gresham was treated at Wilshire Hospital and released."

Her hands were shaking as she turned to the page where the article was continued. "The officers stopped the suspect when he ran a red light, nearly colliding with an ambulance, and the patrolmen gave chase, pulling him over a few blocks from the near-accident. When Paraski requested his license, the suspect pulled a gun from the door pocket, firing point-blank at the officer. Gresham ran toward them, drawing the gunman's attention away from his partner. After firing at Gresham, grazing his left arm, the suspect left the scene and was apprehended on Interstate 80 northwest of Reno. Investigation is continuing."

Joy sat up, her head whirling. What are "minor" injuries when you're shot? What is a "serious but stable" condition? Taking the telephone directory, she turned to the G's, running her finger down the page. No Michael Gresham listed. Of course not. What policeman wants his telephone number where every crackpot can see it? She turned to the hospital listings, finding the number for General Patient Information at Wilshire General. She dialed with shaky fingers.

"How is Corporal Paraski doing?" she asked when a polite voice inquired if she could help.

"As well as can be expected, ma'am," came the expected reply.

She grimaced but pursued it further. "Is he allowed visitors?"

"Yes. Visiting hours are noon till eight in the evening, continuous."

"Thank you."

Mike had invited her to go to headquarters to meet his partner, but now she would meet him sooner than she thought—and she would find out at the same time if Mike was all right.

The paper was left lying on the floor as she made a batch of brownies, popping half a pecan nutmeat into her mouth, pressing the others into the tops of the brownies while they were still warm. She hadn't had breakfast and settled for a glass of milk and two delicious brownies. They should be sampled to ensure they were good enough for Corporal Paraski. They were.

Joy finished reading the paper, fixed a bacon, lettuce and tomato sandwich, and went to dress. Taking special pains with her dress, she checked the three-way mirror to smooth the pale pink linen material over her rounded bottom. The dress was sleeveless with a long-sleeved jacket for the cooler evenings. It was a recent purchase, and she found herself wondering if she had intentionally looked for a quiet color because Ken would like it, as compared to her favorite red.

She shrugged away the thought. Ken was intruding less and less in her thoughts—and about time. But habit was strong, and after all, she was still married to him.

Joy planned her visit late, hoping she would be the last one of the evening to see the injured policeman, or at least not among the daytime rush. It was seven o'clock when she parked in the visitors' parking lot at the hospital, noticing that a lot of the spaces were empty, and she felt a little easier. It was awkward for her to visit a stranger, and the fewer people around, the better.

At the information desk, she was told Corporal

Paraski was in Room 307, and she took the elevator up along with an elderly couple who talked to each other in loud voices and left the elevator ahead of her. An arrow on the wall indicated Rooms 300 through 310 to her left, and she turned down the hallway.

The door was partly open, and Joy hesitated as she looked into the shadowed room. A dim light burned over the table that held a water pitcher, a glass and a box of tissues. There were no other visitors and she breathed a sigh of relief.

Corporal Paraski looked younger than the newspaper picture, his hair was wheat-blond, not dark as she had thought, and the thick mustache was a shade darker than his hair. There were no visible signs of injury.

"Hello." The voice came quietly from the bed.

Only then did she see his eyes were open, and she smiled. "Corporal Paraski, I'm—"

"The Christmas Angel," he said. "I'd know you anywhere."

Surprised at his recognition of her after the one brief glimpse four months ago, she stared into his smiling face. "My name is Joy Strayer. I read about you and Sergeant Gresham in the morning paper. Are you going to be all right?"

"If I tell you I'm dying, will you stay all night with me?" he asked. His voice was strong for a dying man.

She laughed. "Of course, but only if you get your doctor's written statement to that effect." She stepped closer to the bed. "I didn't know if you were allergic to flowers or not, so I baked brownies instead." She held out the box of brownies she'd wrapped in foil with a wide elastic gold ribbon around it without a bow; it looked masculine and suited Corporal Paraski.

"My favorite," he assured her, grinning, his uninjured hand held out for the box. "I'll have to hurry and eat them all before Mike comes in after he gets off at midnight."

"Will they let him in after visiting hours?"

"He won't ask."

"How badly are you hurt?" His left shoulder and arm were bandaged and secured against his chest so that he couldn't move them. A bruise left a discolored swath down his left cheek.

"I'm in terrible pain," he said, his teeth flashing in a wide grin. Then he sobered. "If not for Mike, I'd be dead. Fortunately, his yell broke the guy's concentration on me. One bullet in the shoulder missed the bones, so I'm sore, that's all."

Joy studied the young-looking face. *They face death every day watching out for people like me,* she thought. *No wonder Mike says a policeman's wife has to be tougher than her husband.*

"And Mike?" she asked.

His eyebrows rose. "Mike? How come I'm Corporal Paraski and he's Mike?"

"Well, I..." She could feel the blush in her cheeks, thinking what he'd say if he knew she stayed in Mike's house Friday night. "We played tennis and I beat him, so I couldn't call him sergeant as I was rubbing it in, could I?"

"You beat Mike at tennis?" He shook his head in disbelief, much the same as Paula had done. He blinked, and it seemed to her he was having trouble keeping his eyes open. The nurses had been by with pills, one of which could have been to help him sleep as well as for pain.

"Well, you need your rest now. I'd better go," she said. "I'll open the brownies for you." She took the box and slipped the elastic ribbon from the box, placing them on the table close enough for him to reach. "Good night, Corporal Paraski."

"I'd rather you call me Ski," he said.

At the door, Joy turned to smile at him. "Good night, Ski." Leaving the door partly open, as it had been when she arrived, she walked through empty halls to the elevator, thinking that hospitals were very lonely places.

The cookies and sandwich she had eaten during the day disappeared from her stomach, and she wondered what might be interesting to eat at the apartment. Nothing, she was certain.

She drove down the street past the mall where the Christmas tree had stood and turned left into the street near the coffee shop, pulling into a parking space directly in front of it.

Inside she looked around for Paula and, not seeing her, made her way to the booth she had shared with Mike on Friday night. She looked up as the swinging doors to the kitchen area swung outward and Paula came through balancing a tray in each hand. She served the couple in the booth next to Joy and turned to place a menu in front of her.

"Why, Joy," she said. "How are you?"

"I'm fine. I just came from the hospital."

"You saw Ski? I was there earlier, too." She shuddered. "I know he'll be all right now, but those close calls scare me to death." She took out her pad to write Joy's order. "Don't mention I said that; policemen don't think we should worry about them, you know."

"Have you seen Mike since it happened?"

"No. He has tomorrow off, so he'll probably stop by." Paula wet her pencil in her mouth and prepared to write.

Joy looked unseeingly at the menu, remembering Corporal Paraski's young-looking face and his comment when she asked if the nurses would let Mike in after visiting hours. "He won't ask," he had said. She could well imagine Mike's reaction if they tried to stop him.

"I'll have a cheeseburger with french fries and a strawberry milkshake." She looked up at Paula as she wrote it down. "Doesn't Mike get any time off for his injury?"

The other girl smiled as she took the menu from Joy's hand. "He doesn't consider a break in the skin an injury. That's just enough to make him mad, and woe be to anyone who crosses his path until Ski's back with him."

Joy watched her walk away and, for the first time, wondered if she was Mike's girlfriend. Not what you would term pretty, Paula had an elfin face sprinkled with freckles and reddish-blond hair cut short and worn straight. Her figure in the neat blue-and-white uniform bordered on the voluptuous, and all customers enjoyed her ready smile.

Joy looked down at her hands linked together in front of her on the table. *Everyone needs someone, even Mike,* she thought. *He thinks I'd never be strong enough for someone like him, but I can survive on my own. And alone. Millions of people do it every day.*

Paula brought her order, leaving her with her thoughts as more people came to be served. She ate quickly, waving to Paula as she paid her bill and left the coffee shop. It was nine o'clock.

Her thoughts turned to work the next day, wondering idly what the week held in store. She was due to go to Red Lodge on Wednesday and was looking forward to the trip. She needed supplemental information from the dam site to go along with the expansion figures she'd revamped.

At home, she undressed, pulling a long T-shirt over her head, glancing to see that it was Number 11—Danny White of Dallas Cowboys fame. Bending to pick up the paper she had left scattered on the floor, she saw Corporal Paraski's picture and went for the scissors. She clipped the picture and article, and slipped it into a large album lying on the end table by the couch.

From the living room she went into the small kitchen area to clean, putting away the pan where she had baked the brownies, throwing the dish sponge and towel into her clothes hamper as she passed it. Standing for a moment in the bedroom door, she let her glance rest on the neatly made bed, remembering the tumbled covers of Ken's bed after a shared night of love between them. She winced and went to turn the covers back on the one side where she slept. Tomorrow morning the covers would be disturbed only a little, and she could turn them up over the pillow with a single movement.

A few minutes later, she slipped between the sheets to lie thinking about Mike and Ski. *I can almost believe Mike is right when he says a policeman should never marry.* What woman could ever keep her sanity wondering every morning when she kissed her husband good-bye if he would come home again? A tremendous feeling of sympathy for policemen's wives filled her heart as she drifted into sleep.

Monday morning she dressed in a navy silk pantsuit with a red-and-white polka-dot blouse, a floppy bow tied beneath her chin. Red patent slippers with crepe soles would be comfortable for all the walking she'd need to do in order to get her slides and ledgers ready for her trip. It was eight o'clock when she dialed the hospital and asked for Room 307.

"Hello?" a deep voice questioned.

"Corporal Paraski?"

"Yes."

"It's Joy. How are you this lovely day?" she asked.

"Fine, if you're on your way to see me."

She laughed. "I'm a working girl, Ski. Only the chosen few can lie in bed and be waited on."

"Will you come by to see me after work?" he asked.

"I usually eat lunch around two and thought I'd run

by to see you then, since I have to work late tonight,''
she said.

"Okay."

"Can I bring you anything?"

"Just you, Joy. They take care of my other needs,"
he teased.

It was easy to laugh at him. "See you then."

She hung up the phone and moved through the
apartment, taking her handbag and briefcase from the
table on her way out the door, checking to see it
locked behind her. She ran down the steps to her car
parked in the slot at the side of the apartment, standing for a moment to breathe in the freshness of the
fragrant April morning.

Head back, the cloud of black hair swung over her
shoulders as she stood, legs braced apart, she stared at
the cloudless jewel-blue sky.

It's a day to be happy, she said to herself, *and I have
nothing to mope about—anymore.* So saying, she unlocked her car and slid behind the wheel and a few minutes later turned into Conan Enterprises' property.

At nine, Joy joined Tom and the management executives for a briefing on what they wanted out of Red
Lodge, and at ten-thirty she was back at her desk. The
phone rang and she picked it up while she was still
standing.

"Joy Strayer," she said.

"Hello, Joy."

The familiar deep voice shocked her, and she sat
down abruptly, feeling the blood drain from her face.
"Yes, Ken?"

"How are you?" he asked.

She swallowed and shook her head before she said, "I'm fine." *What's wrong with me?* she wondered. *He's just my husband, soon to be ex.* "How are you and Penny?" She stared at the writing on the ledger in front of her but, had her life depended on it, she couldn't have quoted a word from it.

"All right." She heard his indrawn breath before he went on. "I'd like to see you, Joy. We need to talk."

Divorce papers were being prepared, but she supposed other things came up with people like Ken who studied every detail with a magnifying glass. Her name was probably still on things that needed to be changed.

"Of course, Ken." Her heart slowed from its hurried beat and moment of excitement at hearing his voice. It had been a long time.

"Would tonight be all right? We could go to dinner."

"Yes, that will be fine," she said.

"Seven-thirty?"

"Yes." The work she needed to do for Red Lodge could wait a few hours without suffering.

She heard Ken say, "I'll pick you up at seven-thirty, Joy," and the receiver echoed the click as the connection was broken. She sat there, waiting for the old heartache to start, the old longing and hope that persisted in the first weeks and months after she left Ken's house. It didn't come; all she could think about was what he might say of importance to her at this stage of the game.

Chapter Five

Pulling into a space someone had just pulled out of near the entrance to the hospital, Joy locked her car and ran lightly across the paved area. She was the sole occupant of the elevator going to the third floor. Turning left down the hall, she slowed as she reached Room 307, relieved that the door was open and there were no other visitors.

Ski's eyes were on the door as she half skidded around the door frame, and he grinned, appreciating what he saw.

"I was afraid you'd forget," he said.

She shook her head. "Of course I wouldn't forget about you, Ski," she assured him.

He put out his open hand and she stepped closer to the bed, placing her fingers across it. "Are you getting your strength back?" she asked.

"Enough so that he's up to his old tricks of flirting with all the pretty girls," a voice said behind her.

Startled, Joy half turned, but Ski held on to her hand. "Don't listen to him," he told her. "It's jealousy."

She smiled at the man standing beside her. "Hello, Mike. I'm glad you two were so very lucky." He was in uniform, either on his way for duty or in midshift, neat and straight, his hat tucked under his left arm. He had recently had a haircut and dark gray-sprinkled wings waved back from his tanned face.

For an instant, dark anger turned his eyes black until he blinked, hiding their expression. He smiled as he spoke to Ski. "Hurry up and get out of here. Sorenson's a good kid, but if I have to eat at Godfather's Pizza one more time, I'm going to detail him to Ely for the rest of the year."

"What's wrong with Godfather's Pizza?" she asked.

"Not you, too," he groaned. "Maybe once a month, but twice on every shift? Have a heart, Joy."

Thinking the two friends wanted to talk shop, Joy took her leave. "I have to grab a sandwich and take it back to work and hope the boss doesn't catch me eating at my desk," she said. Yes, if Tom caught her eating at her desk and not taking an hour or more off at lunch, he'd give her his stern health lecture.

"I'll buy you lunch," Mike said. "In part payment for the brownies." He was grinning at her.

"Yeah, he ate most of them while they still had me too doped up to count how many he got." Ski looked with interest at Mike now. "You just got here. You mean that's all the visit I get?"

"Be reasonable, Ski," his friend said. "Given a choice between talking to you and having lunch with Joy, what would you do?"

"Since you put it like that, okay. But make sure you

come back tonight." He lay back against the pillow. "Watch out for him, Joy, he's a sergeant and used to giving orders."

"Mike, I really should get back. I'm going—"

He took her arm, waving to Ski as they went out the door. "You said you had to grab a sandwich," he said. "So we'll grab a sandwich at Paula's. Best and fast."

There was little chance to argue, and she wasn't sure she wanted to anyway. Outside, he stopped by the patrol car parked in a restricted zone.

"Where's your car?"

"There." She pointed. "I'll meet you at the coffee shop."

Mike knew all the shortcuts, and was parked and waiting for her when she arrived. He opened the door, touching her arm as she swung around in the seat and stepped up on the sidewalk.

The lunch crowd had gone, and few people were inside the café as they found a booth near the back. Paula came immediately.

"I don't believe Mike's playing hooky from the war zone," she teased. "And Joy, too?"

"We're on a secret mission," he told her. "And hungry. What's good?"

Paula rattled off all the good things, and Mike said, "Bring us two of whatever you suggest. I've been skipping most of my lunch breaks since Sorenson knows only where Godfather's Pizza is."

Paula wrote something on the ticket and looked at Mike closely. "Have you seen Ski today?"

"Matter of fact, we just came from there. He's looking better." A darkness crossed his face and was gone.

"Yes, he does," Joy said. "A lot better."

Paula nodded and hurried away. Joy wondered what she'd get to eat.

"Do you have to hurry, Joy?"

"If I take an hour, I don't think Tom will fire me. At least not before the Red Lodge project is done." She laughed. "Nobody else can straighten out the mess I've made of those first figures." Tom would probably applaud if he knew she was taking two hours for lunch. She worked enough unrecorded overtime to cover several lunchtimes per week, and he knew it—and disapproved.

"What's the Red Lodge project?" Mike's gaze went over her features. The deep violet-blue of her eyes sparkled now in contrast to how she looked the day he picked her up from a snowy sidewalk. The twin dimples flashed more often, and with more smiles the tip of her tongue played with the uneven front tooth. It was a tantalizing movement, and Mike watched it now as moisture glistened on her lips where her tongue had licked them.

Joy sat back in the booth, unaware of his intense interest in her mouth. "It's a long story."

"I'm on split shift today and don't have to be back on duty till six o'clock."

"What an odd type of duty."

He laughed. "And you haven't heard half of the schedules we have to keep. That's why we have partners, so one of us will remember what time we have to work." He leaned his elbows on the table. "So I have time to hear about Red Lodge. Sounds like a dude ranch."

"Not quite, but there are some around." She told him about the small town in Montana, just across the Wyoming state line from Yellowstone National Park; about the dam scheduled three years ago to be built there to provide power and water reserves to the area; and the subsequent injunction to stop the work.

"And now?"

"Now I have to rework all the figures I submitted back then, taking into consideration inflation hedges, new minimum wage laws, higher prices for materials, higher prices for consultants. Everything's changed."

"And what's your place in all of this?"

"I'm in the middle of it," she said, laughing. "I started out with the first bid for the contract that Conan's submitted, working out the scheduling program for the construction of the dam. I worked with federal agencies to figure the environmental effect, such as endangering wildlife or destroying forests by using space now reserved for them. We found out that by moving the site of the dam a half a mile upstream the wildlife would still have plenty of water and places to cross."

"How are you going to keep from destroying some of the forest?" Mike's quiet gaze never left her face as she talked.

"We have to reseed and replant within ninety days of completion of the dam. It's called reclamation."

"Who guarantees that will be done?"

"I do. I have to order the seedlings, and I have to see that they get to the forestry division that takes care of planting."

He continued to look at her long after she stopped talking, and she could feel the color washing into her face at his steady gaze. To her relief, Paula came back with plates of food that smelled absolutely heavenly. Joy hadn't even thought about being hungry.

"Aren't you going to ask what it is?" Mike asked as she picked up her fork.

She shook her head. "It smells so good, I don't care what it is."

Paula, still standing nearby, laughed. "It's Maude's special meat casserole, mostly beef tips and cheese, Joy. Mike knows we serve it every Monday, and we have to save some for him no matter what time he comes in."

As Paula walked away, Joy smiled across the table. "That's cheating, you know."

He waved his fork. "Eat."

When she leaned back and sighed, he said, "Do you have to go back to work?"

Her eyes, half closed with deep contentment, flew open. She was too surprised to answer him immediately. Ken had interrupted her morning; now Mike threw a monkey wrench into the afternoon. *What* is *this?* she thought.

Before she could gather her thoughts together to give him a sensible answer, he smiled and said, "I saw you horseback riding in the park one day, and since I have a couple of hours between shifts, I thought maybe we could ride for a while."

"When was that?" She rode when she worked until her body and mind were tight from concentrating on figures and the thought of staying indoors one more hour drove her up the wall.

"Just last week. We had a call to the art gallery and were on our way there."

"Was it robbed?" She sat forward, her face lifted to him in interest.

He was smiling, so he wasn't thinking of anything serious. As a matter of fact, what he was thinking at the moment was how much her face lit up with animation when she concentrated on a subject. Her eyes widened and velvety black lashes spread outward with the movement. He could swear the small turned-up nose wiggled.

He shook his head. "A false alarm. We were only there a few minutes, but when we passed the park again, you were gone." He continued to study her uplifted face. "Do you ride often?"

"A couple of times a week when I can."

"You shouldn't ride over on that side of the park alone at that time of day."

"Really, Mike," she said, her voice soft. "I don't have a lot of choice. That is, if I want to ride."

"Call me. I'll ride with you."

Their eyes locked for a long minute, each sizing the other up, neither looking away. Joy finally lost the battle. "I never know your schedule."

"Information will tell you where I am. I'll leave

word." He waited a few seconds as she thought about it. "Okay?"

She gathered up her handbag. "Thanks, Mike. I might do that."

"Sure you have to go back to work?"

"I'm afraid so," she said. "I have only one more day before I go to Red Lodge, and a million and one things to do before I leave."

He nodded. "How are you otherwise?" His expression grew serious. "I mean other than staying too busy to think about the divorce."

The word sent cold chills through her warm body; she hated it. Adjusting the handbag strap over her shoulder, she kept her eyes away from Mike. His question brought her back to thoughts of wondering what Ken had on his mind, and she realized she was more curious than worried, as she might have been at one time.

"Everyone's busy this time of year, Mike. Even you."

"Yeah, you're right. In the spring a young man's fancy and all that, plus all the young women are just as bad." He stood up, placing a bill on the ticket Paula had left on the table. She called good-bye to them as they left, and Joy turned to wave.

At her car, she smiled up at him. "Take care of Ski while I'm gone and go easy on Sorenson. Just remember that pizza has all the natural daily vitamins you need."

He stared at her a moment, then threw back his head and laughed. "I hope Sorenson never finds that

out. I'd never hear the last of it." She had never heard
him laugh; it was a nice sound.

She slid beneath the steering wheel, and Mike
closed the door. She rolled the window down and
dipped her head to look up at him at the same time as
he stooped to lean toward her, and their lips met
briefly. Startled, she felt her pulse leap, and a quick
intake of breath parted her lips. Long fingers slid beneath her hair to curve around her neck, and finger-
tips caressed lightly over the lobe of her ear. She was
drawn closer, and once more, Mike's mouth, firm
and dry, touched hers.

Quickly he released her and straightened up, stepping away from the car. "Take care, Joy."

Automatically she started the car and pulled from
the curb, glancing in the mirror to see Mike looking
after her.

Back at the office, she sat at her desk, ledgers
spread to every corner, staring from one set of figures
to another. Figures that normally did her bidding,
coming up with any number of solutions to complicated problems, could just as well have been hiero-
glyphics for the sense they made to her.

Finally she gave up and went home to dress for
the dinner with Ken, but her mind was on Mike
Gresham.

SHE'S JUST A KID, Mike was thinking as he walked
through the living room, dragging the tie from around
his neck and using one hand to slip the shirt buttons
free. She can't be more than twenty-five, if that. And

what kind of job is that for such a tiny bit of a thing? It sounded complicated to him. He wasn't dumb, but figures were something he used when necessary and at no other time.

Mike Gresham wasn't a male chauvinist, although at times he could sound like one. There were women in the police department, but he'd never been assigned with one. He hoped he never would be. He shied away from the thought of having to watch one faint when she picked up a body from a bloody highway accident, or pulled someone from the river—especially if the victims of cruel accidents were children. Women were too...well, they were too gentle for such things.

His mother would argue like crazy with him. She'd shared the life of a policeman with his father and her father-in-law, and he knew it hadn't been easy. That was an understatement. When you became a policeman's widow at an early age with a young son to raise alone, nothing's easy. He couldn't remember his mother ever complaining, and she made no objection when he chose police work. What her personal thoughts and anxieties had been he could only guess at.

But Joy Strayer was a different story. She'd never talked much about her marriage, only giving the impression she was still somewhat lost. When she'd lost the baby, her eyes held a vacant look the few times he'd seen her, even the day he found her Christmas shopping and took her home with him. He grinned, remembering the way she looked curled up in his big

bed with his pajama top covering her like a blanket.
She had been a big temptation that morning.

Her eyes had changed—an odd color of almost
purple with blue lights. He loved the way they sparkled when she laughed. And her tongue as it covered
the uneven front tooth: someday, he planned to catch
that tantalizing piece of flesh. He frowned, shaking
his head at his nonsensical thoughts.

Setting the radio alarm for four-thirty, he stretched
out on the bed. He recognized the uneasy feeling inside him for what it was: he was beginning to think
too much about Joy Strayer. There was no place in
Mike Gresham's life for her. Furthermore, she was
still confused about her marriage's failure and didn't
need further complications in her life.

What kind of man was Strayer? Why had the marriage failed? Maybe she's cold-natured—not too unusual in women—but remembering the brief kisses,
he somehow couldn't buy that. Had he been abusive
to her? Unbidden anger surfaced at the thought and
his fists clenched. He'd damn well better not ever
touch her!

The last thought brought him up short. It was really
none of his business. Joy Strayer had lived all her life
without him, and she could manage quite well if he
followed his naturally self-defensive instincts and
stayed away from her.

JOY DRESSED with extra-special care, pulling her hair
back to loop it in a loose coil low on her neck, allowing
springy tendrils to curl in front of her ears. The pale

yellow dress was of a clinging jersey material that outlined her curving breasts. A wide leather belt accented her small waist and unpressed pleats cascaded over her hips to end just below her knees. Her sandals were gold kid with four-inch heels that added to her height. The doorbell rang as she smoothed a light peach color on her lips.

For a moment, she panicked at seeing Ken again. She had done so well the past two months, and being this close to him could undo all her brave resolutions to put him completely in the past. She fumbled with the lock a little, finally releasing it, and pulled the door open to face Ken.

He stared at her, his eyes approving the paleness of her dress, a contrast to her favorite vivid colors.

"Come in, Ken."

He walked past her, turning as she closed the door. "Joy." He reached to pull her into his arms. "Sweetheart," he whispered. "I've missed you so." His lips touched her forehead and fingers caught her chin to tilt it, and she trembled as he kissed her.

She stayed within the circle of his arms, waiting for the fire Ken could always rouse in her. What she felt instead was a deep regret that they'd never been able to work out their problems.

She cleared her throat and moved away from Ken. "I'm ready to go." His kiss had surprised her, but it shouldn't have. Ken thought he could solve anything by making love to her; something she'd always enjoyed and the only way she'd ever satisfied him.

"You look wonderful, Joy," Ken said, still standing where she'd moved from his arms.

She didn't turn. "Thank you, Ken." Stiffly she walked beside him out to the car, relaxing a little as he talked about Penny and his work. She looked up when the car stopped, to see the small intimate restaurant that had been one of their favorites for Italian food.

Ken linked his arm in hers, pulling her close to his side as he helped her from the car. Inside the candlelit restaurant, they were immediately taken to a table he'd reserved. He ordered their favorite wine without asking and looked across at her.

"Penny thought you'd call her," he said, his voice barely accusing her of neglect.

She unfolded the heavy linen napkin and spread it in her lap. "I thought it best if I didn't intrude anymore." Penny had never really accepted Joy as Ken's wife, although she hadn't tried to replace her mother. It was just that living alone with Ken so many years in the quiet shadows of a long illness, Penny had lost any outgoing traits she might have had. Joy's boisterous exuberance and love of life had met with disapproval from Ken, and through association, Penny disapproved also. In two years, they had calmed her down to a point, but beyond that, she was still the effervescent spirit out to enjoy what life had to offer.

Ken gave their dinner orders, then leaned toward her. "I want you to come back, Joy. We miss you."

She hadn't expected that and she stared, disconcerted. "The divorce papers are already being prepared, Ken. Why did you wait this long?"

He smiled his tolerant smile. "I thought you'd have whatever was bothering you out of your system by now."

"What was bothering me? Look, Ken, you're the one who always found fault with everything I did. What I wore, my hair, the color of my eyes." She shook her head. "I can't change everything to please you and still be an individual."

"When you're married, there are no more individuals, Joy. It's what's best for everyone, not just you."

Funny, he had kept his individualism, his love for Sharon and Penny aside from what he felt for her. But Joy had to give hers up. Years in the orphanage had left her with a wish to belong to someone, someone who was hers alone, and sharing him with a dead woman didn't fit what she wanted. She'd loved Ken and Penny. She stopped, realizing her thoughts put them in the past tense.

Platters of food were placed in front of them and they ate, but Joy never tasted anything. Ken gave his reasons for wanting her back, reasons the divorce should be abandoned.

"Your problem was that you were jealous of Sharon and—"

She caught her breath. "Ken, no—"

"And Penny. You couldn't accept—"

She stood up. "Please take me home, Ken." Without waiting, she turned and walked from the restaurant. When he joined her at the car, he was obviously upset.

"You see, Joy, this is the type of thing you do without listening to my side at all. We can work this out."

She didn't answer him. Work what out? As far as Ken was concerned, there was no problem. There had been a time when she'd have tumbled back into his arms without question, but she'd lived away from him long enough to know that she didn't want Ken on his terms. And Ken would never change.

He left her, still arguing that they should try again, that he'd help her adjust. The three of them would do things together; they could redecorate Sharon's house....

She slammed the door closed behind Ken and whirled to look at the room in front of her. Ken had been in it once before when he brought some of her books she'd left behind.

"It certainly is small," he'd said. "What are you going to do with these?" He indicated the three boxes of books he'd placed on the floor.

It was small, but it was hers. She found a place for the books, caressing the well-used bindings. They found no fault with Joy, and she certainly never complained about them. She found satisfaction with the books, something she'd never done with Ken.

One more day and I can get out of Reno for a while, she thought now. One more day. It was early and she pulled out a ledger to look at it, concentrating on a new map Cliff had drawn up for her. The only difference from the one they'd used three years earlier was in the location of the dam, a half mile upriver from the old spot.

She ran her finger along the thin green line alongside the marked stream. The higher elevations would still have snow on them at this time of year, but it should be much more pleasant in the valley.

I wish Tom was going with me, she thought, kicking off her slippers and sitting at the table. She grinned. If Tom knew she was still going over these papers, he'd threaten to fire her.

Chapter Six

"Weather will be in the mid-fifties under mostly clear skies—"

Joy turned off the radio in the rented car she was driving and turned the fan on the heater up a notch. It might be in the mid-fifties later in the day, but it was cold as blue blazes right now. She drove past the Yellowstone County Historical Museum and the impressive "Range Rider of the Yellowstone," a monument to early settlers, standing watch over the city of Billings and the Yellowstone Valley.

Wide-open Montana countryside stretched ahead of her, and she turned her thoughts to the detailed work she had ahead of her for Conan Enterprises. Besides the work, she had to allay any fears of the people in Red Lodge about Conan's ruining their valley and leaving them with the danger of flooding. There was a lot of snow to melt and run off from the mountains, and the dam had better be in a strategic spot to take care of it. Tom Conan paid her well to know her business, and he expected her to satisfy the townspeople as well as Conan Enterprises.

The dam site was deserted when she pulled up to the place she and Tom had inspected not long ago. As agreed, a lot of clearing had been done, and she took notes as she walked the area, coming to the busy stream to stand gazing at the water. It rushed over boulders and trunks of huge trees that had fallen in nature's assaults over the years.

A tributary siphoned off the Yellowstone River. It was beautiful, a serenity few people witness in the quiet of an early spring day. In Reno, the rush would be on for those who worked for a living. For those who played at the casinos, the rush would continue as usual.

She turned as the sound of a motor hummed through the hush of solitude she was enjoying. A long-bed pickup truck, marked Carlisle Construction, stopped a few yards away from her, and she walked toward it as a man got out and strode to meet her.

He grinned as he came closer. It was Gage Carlisle, one of the foremen who had attended their meetings with the town council in Red Lodge.

"'Morning," he said, removing his glove and extending his hand. She did the same.

"Good morning, Gage."

"Are you here alone?" he asked, his glance sweeping the area around them. He wore a red insulated jacket, and a wool knit cap was pulled over his ears. The face he turned to her had weathered perhaps fifty years of this climate, and squint lines spread from dark eyes as he looked down at her.

She smiled. Tom had been with her the last time

she talked to him, and like most men, Gage thought a small, feminine person like Joy was best used for scenery. She enjoyed surprising people with her ability, but sometimes it got tedious, convincing them she could do something besides cook and keep her long fingernails polished.

"Yes, I'm alone, Gage," she said now. "I need to get more readings on the widest point of construction. Judging from your clearing progress here, you won't have much trouble with deadlines."

His gaze went from her face to the cloud-specked sky, watching for a moment as the cottony fluffs sailed ahead of a brisk wind. He shook his head. "We have some more bad weather to wait out yet. The past week was a real streak of good luck."

She nodded, well aware of spring's fickle actions in this part of the country. Most roads farther west and south into Yellowstone Park and Beartooth Plateau wouldn't be open to traffic for another month because of ice and heavy snows. Joy had driven south on the highway into Ayo once in early October, entranced by the unbelievable scenery there, but days later a blizzard had closed that same area for a week.

"Do you have a crew coming today?" she asked.

"Later. They started at Pryor this morning and will be here this afternoon." He faced her. "How long you plan to be here?"

"Till tomorrow afternoon. I meet with the mayor and the town council tonight and complete my notes afterward for you and Mr. Conan. That's all I have to do."

Gage grunted. "Good. Give the mayor enough work to keep him busy and out of my hair for a day or two."

She laughed, remembering Mayor Sangen's enthusiasm about the coming boost to employment in the area. Better than hostility, she wanted to tell Gage, but she made sympathetic sounds that he accepted with a reluctant grin.

She pulled out her notebook, sticking her right-hand glove into her jacket pocket and leaving the left one on. Standing there near the water, she had her doubts about the mid-fifties temperature forecast. Maybe in the direct sunshine, but not on the river-bank.

"What I need to do is check the widest part of the construction, Gage. From there I'll have to compare the mouth of the river to the last curve affected by the dam." She pointed to the southeast. "Would you say it's a good two miles from top to bottom?"

"More like two and a half, Joy. You see, you have three jutting portions going behind those low ranges there. You have to allow for the curvature."

"Okay. I see that." She pulled her small calculator from another jacket pocket, pushing buttons and writing down results. "How does that look to you?"

He took the notebook she'd written in, studying the page for several minutes. With the new figures, she'd moved outward from the original boundaries by three feet. It didn't sound like much, but when you counted costs for stone, cable, cement, time and labor, plus reclamation of the land after the dam was completed, it added sixteen days and another two hundred thousand dollars to the cost estimates.

The man beside her didn't hurry, and she studied the rough features as she waited for him to speak. Dark eyes lifted from the page, and he let his gaze run from the highest mountain peak to their north, along the deep cut of the river to the south. His lips moved, and she knew he was juggling her figures around in his head, putting them in place with his own estimates. Men like Gage Carlisle seldom used computers and calculators. Long years of experience in handling giant-sized projects such as this one, dealing with the capricious ways of nature in the process, taught them to come remarkably close to the final cost.

He handed her the notebook and grinned, shaking his head. "I'd say you're within ten thousand dollars, either side of the cost run, Joy. Good calculation."

Tom would be elated if her figures came that close, Joy knew. There were so many things that could change without warning, plus the weather in this country had to be given serious consideration. But if they could get started within the next few weeks, they could get a lot of the preliminary preconstruction of the dam done before the first snow in late fall or early winter.

"How about lunch in Red Lodge, Joy?" Gage asked as they walked back toward where she'd parked. "They have the best stuffed flounder in the state, fresh out of our unpolluted streams."

"Sounds great, but won't it take you away from

your work?" As far as Joy was concerned, she had enough new information—combined with the research she had completed during the trip with Tom—to support her presentation to the council.

"We have to eat a nourishing meal before we can work proper," he assured her. "Mind riding in the truck?"

"I'd better not leave the rented car here. Let's take it."

"Okay."

She turned the car around, and drove the gravel road back to the main highway, turning south toward Red Lodge. A sign gave the distance they still had to drive as sixteen miles. It was a slow sixteen miles, filled with zigzag curves and sharp inclines. It was only eleven o'clock and they were in no hurry, not minding their slow progress as they talked easily about the scenic views. Both enthusiastic about the coming advantages of the dam, they carried their conversation into the cheerful dining room of the Red Lodge Café.

A smiling waitress came to seat them in a roomy booth and placed menus in front of them. "Well, Gage, you just had breakfast," she said. "They must be working you hard these days to bring you back before dinnertime."

Joy looked across at the foreman and smiled as he colored beneath the tanned skin. He cleared his throat. "Must be one of my hungry days, Nan. I decided the stuffed flounder might not be as good tonight."

Nan laughed, took their orders, and moved away. Joy didn't mention Gage's earlier meal; it delighted her to think he wanted to share more time than necessary with her. It was to her benefit to have the site foreman on her side.

"The outdoors must make you hungry," she said. "I'm starved."

Gage relaxed, losing his embarrassment, and they carried on their discussion as though they'd known each other for years. The flounder was as good as promised, and she accepted the offer of hot apple cobbler, groaning in well-filled misery when she finished.

She looked across the table at Gage. "I need to find a room for tonight, and since Conan's picks up the tab, I might as well try the Yodeler."

He grinned. "Great choice. You can call from here."

Nan directed her to a phone, and a few minutes later, her reservation confirmed, Joy returned to the booth. Gage was standing, talking to two men, one of whom she recognized as Mayor Sangen.

"Mrs. Strayer. Nice to have you back," the mayor said. "My comptroller, Max Gardner. We'll see you at six for dinner."

She nodded to them, and they went on to a table at the back as she and Gage left the café. Outside the winds were stronger, and she took her white knit cap from her pocket and pulled it down over her ears, mostly to keep the heavy black hair from blowing every which way. Gage put his cap on as they walked to her car.

"I'll check in at the motel and leave my luggage while we're here, Gage, if that's okay with you."

"Sure," he said.

Joy drove the few blocks to the motel, checked in at the desk, then drove around the side of the building. Gage removed her overnighter from the trunk and set it inside the door for her.

Taking the road back out of Red Lodge toward the site, she pointed to the small stream that ran through the town. "How will our work affect this?" she asked.

"Not at all. The tributary from the Yellowstone branches off, and this creek comes from the lake just below the mountain where we start."

"Good. It's beautiful just like it is." She sighed. "I ate too much and the heater in here makes me sleepy."

"We'll walk down the other side of the river and that'll wake you."

By the time they had finished walking on both sides of the water where they would be working, stepping off approximate widths and lengths of the area, Joy's legs were beginning to notice the unaccustomed activity.

"I'd better get to my room and rest before tonight, or I'll sleep through the speeches," she told him.

"Won't miss much" came Gage's laconic reply. "The only new information will be what you give."

"Well, I'm the one who's supposed to furnish the facts and figures, Gage. I'd be disappointed if someone stole my thunder." She rocked back on her boot heels and grinned at him.

He gave her a reluctant smile and nodded. "I guess so." It was plain he'd rather deal with her than with the mayor.

"I'll see you tomorrow, Gage," she told him as she was leaving. "I'll keep my notes clear so you'll know what I tell them tonight." Gage chose not to attend the "ritzy" gathering with the mayor and the town council.

He waved as she drove off, turning to his truck, but he was still looking after her when she glanced in the rearview mirror.

He probably wonders what in the world somebody like me is doing here and whether I know what I'm doing, she thought, and laughed out loud. He was not the first to have doubts about a half-pint woman knowing anything about figures that related to the construction of mammoth projects such as the Red Lodge dam. What was it Mike called her? A little twerp. A little twerp beating a big, rough cop at tennis. One who was not accustomed to being defeated at anything, especially by a *little* woman. She was still smiling as she pulled into the motel parking slot with her room number.

Inside the pleasantly heated motel room, she removed her cap and heavy coat and kicked off her boots, stretching her tired legs. Obeying previous orders, she placed a call to Tom Conan.

"Well, Joy, how're the wide-open spaces?" he asked, and she could see him smiling.

"Chilly," she told him. "They predict snow tomorrow night, and I hope they're right about the time. It's beautiful, but I really don't care to be stranded here."

"Take an earlier plane out," he said, then went on to business. "What does it look like?"

"All the clearing we agreed on has been done except for the extreme western portion. Gage Carlisle was out there this morning, and he's satisfied with everything. I told him I'd give him my notes after the meeting tonight."

"Good." He hesitated. "Are you all right?"

"Tired, but all right," she assured him, ignoring the fact that she knew he was referring to heartache rather than physical aches. She didn't have to sidestep any issues with Tom. "I'll call you from home tomorrow evening if you're gonna be around."

His voice was dry as he said, "I'll be around, Joy." He was a much-sought-after man, she knew, several years a widower and eligible in capital letters. *If I were twenty years older, I'd take him out of circulation myself,* she thought.

Shaking away the thoughts that led nowhere, she opened her small overnight case. Taking out the dress she planned to wear to the meeting that night, she shook the folds from it and reached for a hanger. It was an off-white wool jersey with long, tight sleeves buttoned halfway to the elbow. On the left side of the top, a small deep red rose was appliquéd, and all around the bottom of the skirt, bigger roses swung on a thin green thread. Shoes and bag matched the roses, and she carried the red velveteen jacket over her arm to prevent wrinkling.

She opened the briefcase and lined up her notes the way she wanted to present her information, replacing them and snapping the case closed. There was only half an hour left till she had to dress, and she spent it doing stretching exercises, then took a long time in the shower.

JOY WALKED into the conference room of the Red Lodge City Hall at five minutes before six and was greeted by a moment of silence, followed by a burst of applause. She stopped in surprise, feeling hot color rush to her face as she looked around the predominantly male gathering.

Mayor Sangen came forward. "Ladies and gentlemen, Joy Strayer of Conan Enterprises." He turned to Joy and smiled. "I hope we didn't embarrass you. It's just that it's been a long, cold winter, and most of our speakers do not, in any way, resemble you, and it's a welcome change." There was another round of applause, and Joy smiled as she pulled her notes from her briefcase.

"Thank you. I'm sorry to disillusion you, but what I have to say is probably as dull in content as most speeches are." With the friendly laughter, she relaxed and went over the facts and figures, answering questions in a straightforward way as they were posed to her.

Mayor Sangen rose to speak as she sat down. "Joy has answered our biggest questions satisfactorily, that of employment and the effect on our environment," he said quietly. "It will be a most welcome boost to our economy, and I hope we can all work together for the best outcome."

They adjourned for the dinner catered at the city hall, and Joy sat with Mayor Sangen and Max Gardner.

"Will you be here all day tomorrow, Joy?"

"No. The only flight out of Billings leaves at two, and I'm hoping to get out ahead of the forecasted snow."

"Don't pay attention to the weatherman," Max said. "It may be Sunday before that snow arrives."

"I can't take the chance," she said, smiling at him, wondering at the same time why she cared if she was stranded or not. No one would miss her, unless she didn't get home Monday and report to Tom.

She said her good-byes early, feeling she had the people of Red Lodge on Conan's side and happy the job would bring a much-needed economic boost to the area.

Friday morning, Joy dressed in a layered outfit that she could partially shed once she was back in Billings, and she drove to the dam site. Gage Carlisle was there ahead of her.

The wind coming out of the mountains was cold, and they sat in the cab of the truck while she went over the few changes the town council had asked for.

Gage nodded with satisfaction. "They're getting better. Usually they pick plans apart and change bits and pieces till everybody's confused." He gave her a big grin. "Tom Conan's smart, sending someone like you." He held up his hand as he saw the sparkle in her eyes. "You know what you're doing, too, which helps." He shook his head. "But when someone looks like you, it's easier to convince the doubters."

Laughing with him, she said, "Okay, Gage, but just you remember, I'm on your side. And I'd better get out of here if I plan to catch that plane."

Driving back along Route 212, turning onto Route 90 toward Billings, she thought of her two days' work. It had brought the results Tom wanted, and work could start as soon as the weather cooperated, hopefully within a few weeks. At the airport, she turned in the rented car and went into the ladies' room to remove her insulated jacket, poking her knit cap into the pocket, and rolled it tight enough to fit into her bag. She checked it through and received her boarding pass.

When her flight was called, Joy followed several others into the plane and had the misfortune of being seated with a nonstop talker. The woman was fashionably dressed, her gray hair neatly coiffed, but her one thought was her physical well-being. After hearing about the removal of her gallbladder last year and the ensuing headaches, Joy surmised that whether she answered the woman or not was irrelevant and contented herself with an occasional murmur of acknowledgment. When the airplane wheels dropped preparatory to landing in Denver, she breathed a sigh of relief, praying the woman would stay in Denver and not go on to Reno.

Her indiscreet prayers were evidently answered as she boarded the flight for Reno, looking around apprehensively to determine who would be her seatmate. The plane was full, and she gratefully sat next to a young couple totally engrossed in each other.

As she sat there, waiting for the plane to lift off the runway, she thought of Mike Gresham, whose mother lived in Denver. "I'd like to take you home to meet my mother," he'd said. She smiled a little, thinking of the serious-minded policeman who thought women were too weak to marry anyone in his field. *All marriages are as weak as the weakest partner, Mike, and policemen's wives are no different.*

The flight was without incident, and she even dozed a few minutes, coming wide awake when the flight attendant announced "Fasten Seat Belts" for the descent into Reno. It was a good feeling to pick up her own car from the long-term parking lot and drive through the familiar streets to her apartment. The weather was a pleasant sixty-five degrees, and it was seven-thirty. She wondered if the snow had arrived as predicted in Red Lodge.

Chapter Seven

The familiar street where she lived had never looked so good, and she realized she was tired. She needed to do more walking if this was any indication.

Unlocking the door to her apartment, she let the door swing inward and placed her bag and briefcase on the floor, reaching for her two-day accumulation of mail from her box before pushing the door closed and locking it. She sniffed, wrinkling her nose at the musty smell that goes with an unlived-in apartment, threw her mail on the table, and raised her bedroom window a fraction to let in fresh air. She stripped off her clothes, placing them in the hamper on her way to grab a light blue silk robe to wrap around her.

In the small kitchen she poured a glass of orange juice and sat down by the telephone to call Tom. When he answered, she smiled as she said, "I'm home."

"About time. How did the meeting go last night?"

"It was productive," she said, and proceeded to relate her total findings at Red Lodge and the reception her presentation got from the town council.

He grunted his satisfaction when she finished. "You need any time off, Joy?"

"No, thank you." She didn't pretend not to know what he meant. They had been friends too long to mince words with each other, and Tom of all people knew she still had her "down" days.

With a promised "I'll see you Monday," she hung up and leafed through the accumulation of letters for "Occupant" and an invitation to an open house at one of Conan's projects in South Lake Tahoe, leaving only a brown, legal-sized envelope to open.

"I wish they'd stop sending me all those sweepstakes notifications that say, 'You may have won two hundred and fifty thousand dollars,' and send me the money instead," she said aloud, turning the letter over to look at the return address. Instead of a Publisher's Clearing House label, there was the name of a familiar Reno law firm.

Slowly she slid her fingernail under the gummed flap, lifting it to remove the expensive stationery from inside. The top half unfolded, and she read: Divorce Decree—Strayer v. Strayer.

The letter slid from her nerveless fingers and slithered down the silky folds of her robe to lie innocently against her bare foot. She stared at the cream-colored paper for a long time while a confusion of emotions charged through her. She thought she was ready for this; she knew it was only a matter of time before the petition was due; she knew... And yet it was like a physical blow without warning, leaving an empty, strangling sensation in her chest.

She didn't think of Ken; she thought only of herself, who had already been through the pain of losing. This was the final commitment to that loss.

Leaving the letter where it had fallen, she got up and went to the small china cabinet in the dinette area. Her hands, reaching inside, rested on a bottle, and she withdrew it to stand looking at the label, a bottle of Rémy Martin cognac Tom had given her for Christmas several years ago. When she left Ken, she took it with her, although she seldom drank anything stronger than wine.

This was a good time to use it, to celebrate the end and the beginning. She broke the gold metallic seal on the bottle and took a water glass from the cabinet above the sink. Walking back into the living room, she stood a moment gazing at the letter she had dropped near the chair, turned and sat down on the floor, leaning back against the big hassock, the bottle and glass still in her hand, the orange juice forgotten. Like someone in a dream, she removed the top from the bottle and poured the glass half full of the amber liquid, recapping the bottle and propping it against the hassock.

Holding the glass up to the light, she smiled and said, "To us, Ken. Not together, but, from this day, may we have better luck apart." Taking a big swallow, she gasped as it all but took away her breath. She coughed and gagged, wiping tears from her eyes. A few seconds later, the next swallow went down more easily, and the ones after that were no trouble at all.

The ringing penetrated the fog she was in, and she stared at the phone without moving. The ring had a strange sound to it, she thought, and decided she'd better answer it in case it was someone she knew. She giggled. Of course, if they were calling her, they must know her, right? Right.

Carefully, she placed the glass on the carpet and struggled to her feet just as the ringing stopped, to be replaced by a thunderous pounding on her door. Both hands went to her head where the sound echoed and reechoed.

"All right, all right," she muttered, standing straight and trying to engage her legs in motion.

"Joy?"

She frowned, trying to identify the vaguely familiar voice. Unsuccessful in doing so, she moved one foot in front of the other with exaggerated exactness, finally reaching the door.

"Who—" She hiccuped and started over. "Who is it?"

"Mike. Open the door, Joy."

Her fumbling fingers caught the latch, sliding it back, and as she did so, the door was pushed open. She stumbled backward to lean against the wall as Mike stepped through the doorway.

He sent a quick glance around the room before he really looked at her, gray eyes darkening to black as they took in the cloud of tumbled hair and half-closed blue eyes. His gaze went down the silk robe clinging to her slim figure, opened almost to her waist to expose the soft curves of her breasts.

His eyes narrowed and his voice deepened with his accusation. "You're drunk."

She leaned her head back against the wall, staring at him with a solemn expression till, suddenly, she grinned, dimples appearing in both cheeks. She wagged an unsteady finger at him.

"But I'm not driving, Mike, so you can't... can't arrest me for... for driving under... under the influence." She straightened away from the wall and took a step toward him, not in the least intimidated by his angry expression. "Have a drink, Mike. I'm c-celebrating."

His hands came out slowly and caught her arms. "What the hell are you celebrating alone?"

She tilted her head back to look at him, frowning into his angry eyes. "I—I don't remember."

He continued to hold her, gazing at the sweet curve of her mouth, and slowly his arms went around her, his head bent, and he placed his mouth on hers. The blue eyes, only half-opened, closed now and silky lashes dropped to hide the uncertainty he read there. She answered the kiss, pressing her body into his, moving her lips until they parted as he plundered ruthlessly inside the opening. She held on tightly.

When his mouth finally released hers, he looked into wide-open eyes, sparkling like distant stars, and he drew in a shaky breath.

"Tell me what happened, Joy," he said softly, feeling the tantalizing curves of her body through her robe.

She shook her head, her eyes on his mouth. "I

don't know." She leaned away from him. "I need another drink."

"No," he told her, hands again tight on her arms. "You've just come back from Red Lodge, haven't you?"

After thinking about that question, she nodded. "Yes."

"You're going to tell me what happened, or I'll shake you to bits."

The dimples flashed again. "I'll give you a drink, Mike," she bargained. "One for you and one for me." She gave him a confident smile at her ability to figure that one out. "Deal?"

"No deal," he told her. "What are you drinking?"

She peered around him and pointed toward the hassock where the bottle rested at a forty-five-degree angle. "It's good, Mike. And—and it only takes a little bit to make you for-forget whatever's b-bothering me." She frowned. "Bothering you." She shook her head, giving him a dimpled smile. "See? I don't even remember who's bothered."

Mike could have told her who was bothered, and without the benefit of the first drink. Drawing her with him to the couch, he pushed her down onto the cushions, and as he turned away to reach for the bottle, his foot hit the letter. He picked it up, preparing to place it on the table when she sucked in her breath. He looked around at her to see her eyes fastened on the paper in his hand. Her stricken gaze lifted to meet his, and her parted lips trembled until she bit into them.

Unfolding the letter, he read a few lines, his eyes going quickly to her white face, then back to the letter, which he read all the way through. When he finished, he folded it back into its original shape and placed it on the end table near a glass of untouched orange juice.

"Weren't you expecting this?" he asked.

"Yes." She stiffened and her chin went up defiantly.

"Are you still in love with him? Is that why you're trying to drown your troubles?"

"I told you. I'm celebrating."

"Yeah, I can see that," he said, and smiled.

She got to her feet, swaying a little. "I want a drink." She stared at him in defiance. "If you won't drink with me, I'll drink alone."

"Sit down, Joy, I'll get us a drink."

She sat down, her back straight, watching as he took another water glass from the cabinet and picked hers up from the floor, filling each one to the halfway mark. When he finished, he held the bottle up to the light to see how much was left in it, and as he put it down on the table near the letter, he said, "You're going to have one helluva hangover tomorrow."

"Will it hurt?"

"I'm afraid so," he said, smiling as he handed her the glass.

She turned the glass around in her hand and held it up to touch his. "Here's to future hurts. From this day, may they all be hurts of the head, not the heart." She took two big gulps before she put the glass down and shivered as the liquor burned its way down her throat.

"That's not the way to get over anything, Joy," he said.

She nodded. "I know that, Mike, but right now it seems the best way to cushion the shock." She glanced at him from beneath heavy lashes. "Yes, I know it shouldn't have been a shock, but somehow, even after all this time, even knowing..." She let her voice trail off.

"You still have to face the facts, now or tomorrow."

"I have. I'm all right, Mike, really." She leaned back against the cushions and as she closed her eyes the room swayed. She reached for the glass, and when Mike placed it in her hand, she turned to smile at him.

"What brings you to my side of town on Friday night?"

"Ski gets out of the hospital tomorrow morning, and he wanted you to come to his welcome-home party tomorrow night."

She thought of Ski, so dangerously near death but for the split-second timing of Mike's yell that broke the gunman's concentration. Life is such a delicate commodity, and death is so final. *I'm drunk,* she thought. *All drunks get philosophical.*

"If I'm sober, I'll be there," she said, taking a swallow of the cognac. "You'd better tell me where he lives."

"I'll come get you," he said. "You'll never remember any directions I'd give you tonight."

She nodded and sighed. "I'm sleepy."

"You're drunk."

"That too," she admitted.

He framed her face with both hands and kissed the closed eyes, trailing light touches down her cheek until his mouth covered hers. The tip of his tongue entered tentatively and as her lips parted, he probed gently this time, tasting the drink in her mouth. Moving his hands downward, he followed her curves, easy to feel through the soft material of her robe, and tightened his hold at her small waist.

He lifted his head to look into her wide-open eyes. "I thought you were sleepy."

She smiled. "You underestimate your kisses, Mike."

He kissed her cheek and stood up, lifting her easily, and carried her into the bedroom, placing her on top of the old red chenille spread.

"Can you manage to get yourself to bed?" he asked.

"Yes, thank you," she said, her voice polite as though to a nice stranger.

"Where are your nightgowns? I could lay one out for you so you wouldn't have to stoop over."

She was looking up at him and saw the sympathetic smile on his face and the tenderness she'd not seen in a long time. "I'll do it."

"Good night, Joy, I'll pick you up at eight tomorrow evening."

"All right." Joy watched him leave her and heard the front door close behind him. She turned to bury her face in the pillow and went to sleep, leaving the light on.

HER FIRST THOUGHT on awakening was to the effect that whatever she did was going to be wrong. She turned over and her head rolled sideways, throbbing to the beat of a million drums, proving her first thought.

Cognac is expensive, she thought blearily; *it should leave a pleasant aftereffect.*

Why was I drinking cognac, she wondered. And remembered. She lay still for a long time, aching eyes focused on a cobweb swinging lazily in the corner of the room. She never thought of dusting ceilings until she lay in bed and saw the results of neglect. It didn't bother her.

So what about the day after the night before, Joy? So, Ken is in the past, and Joy, alone, is in the future. I might as well get started on it and see where it leads.

Carefully she sat up, waiting until the room stopped spinning before she moved her legs over the edge of the bed. Her mouth was so dry it crackled, or maybe the noise was her hair breaking into tiny pieces as it swung on her shoulders. She thought longingly of the pitcher of cold orange juice in the refrigerator, despairing of ever making a trip that far all in one day.

What day was it? Saturday. Thank goodness. Tom Conan would have conniptions if his marketing consultant walked into the office still half-lit. From his cognac, yet.

Her eyelids felt swollen, and she couldn't see the hands on her watch to see what time it was. *I don't have to go anywhere, so why torture myself?* She let her body down on the bed as easily as she could and stretched her trembling legs. A glare hurt her eyes, and she put her hands over them to shut out the room light, still on from the night before.

The ringing of the phone penetrated her fog of pain, and she groaned, deciding immediately that whoever it was could call back at a more convenient time. But he or she was persistent, and as the phone rang on and on, she dragged herself up and staggered blindly toward the living room. The bedroom door was open, luckily, and she wasn't forced to waste precious energy opening that, wondering vaguely why she'd left it that way.

She sat down carefully, reaching for the phone, tempted to sling the noisy instrument as far as she could send it. On the table lay the divorce papers, and she turned her head so she wouldn't have to look at them.

"Hello?" she said, her voice thin because of the dryness in her mouth. She held her head with her free hand.

"Joy?" She winced as Mike's deep voice vibrated through the instrument in her hand.

"Yes."

"How do you feel?" he asked.

"As soon as you hang up, I'm going to die," she told him, and heard him laugh as a sudden thought hit her. "How did you know I wouldn't feel good?"

He hesitated, then asked, "Don't you remember that I was there?"

"No. Oh." A dim recollection came to her. "Yes.

Yes, barely, but I do seem to remember your being there...here."

"Have you eaten anything?" he asked.

Her stomach lurched at the thought, and she moaned. "No."

"I'm off duty. I'll be over shortly to fix you something," he said.

"Just bring a basket of pansies. I'll be dead before you get here."

He laughed at her. "You'll live, Joy. Go take a cold shower, and I'll be there in half an hour."

Chapter Eight

Replacing the receiver, she sat still, trying to remember Mike being with her. Dimly she recalled his arms around her and for the first time realized she was still wearing the robe she had put on as soon as she got in from her trip. And something else: the strength of his body through the soft material.

Then what, she wondered and gave up trying to recall any more details.

The idea of a cold shower appealed to her, but her body was a leaden weight with no get-up-and-go to it. She was still sitting by the phone, eyes resolutely ignoring the papers lying nearby, when the doorbell rang. She winced at the shrill sound but managed to stand without too much of a struggle, gathering her robe more closely around her as she went to the door.

As she turned the knob, the door swung inward, and she looked up at Mike, blinking at the bigness of him filling the opening. She stepped back to let him in.

"I wasn't expecting you so soon," she murmured,

embarrassed at having on the same robe she'd worn the night before and slept in. But at least it was a robe and not her favorite Number Eleven T-shirt.

"I said half an hour and it's been thirty-five minutes," he said, smiling down at her.

She pushed the door closed and leaned against it. "You're very prompt."

"Feel rough?" he asked, sympathy in his voice.

"I'm serious when I tell you I don't think I'll survive."

"A shower would help if you think you can manage it. I'll help you."

She made a small negative movement with her head, and even so, it rattled her teeth.

He put an arm around her, guiding her back to the couch. "Sit here a few minutes, and I'll scramble some eggs for you." His glance went to the envelope, but he didn't mention it.

"No, please," she protested.

"You have to eat. When was your last meal?"

She shrugged with lack of interest. "I had a Coke and peanuts on the plane yesterday afternoon."

He made a noise that was probably swearing, but he released her arm and went into the kitchen where she could hear him moving around. In no time it seemed, he came in with a plate of scrambled eggs and toast, handing her a napkin at the same time. He sat beside her, holding a knife and fork.

"What time is it?" she asked, trying to put off that inevitable first bite.

"One-thirty." He handed her the utensils.

She stared at him, disbelief in her face. "What are you doing off duty?"

"I went to work at five this morning." He watched her. "Eat," he said.

Obediently, she put the fork into the fluffy eggs and managed to get it into her mouth, swallowing with difficulty. She looked up at him.

"Why do you bother?"

"It's no bother, and you obviously need some help."

"But you don't owe me anything."

"No," he admitted.

He met her glance, and she looked away from the penetrating gray of his eyes and took a few more small bites. She started to rise, and he took the plate from her.

"Is that all you can eat?"

"Yes."

He came back from the kitchen after depositing the dishes in the sink. "Now for the shower."

She shook her head. "I want to go back to bed."

"No," he said. "If you can't manage on your own, I'll do it for you." His voice coaxed her the way he might do a rebellious child.

"Just go away, Mike, and I'll be okay."

"You promised to go to Ski's homecoming party tonight, and you won't make it if you don't move around."

She squinted at him. "I won't even be able to walk by tonight."

He reached, pulling her up and supporting her.

"You wouldn't disappoint him, would you, Joy? He's counting on your being there."

If Ski could risk his life every day, and almost lose it, and he wanted her at his party, well, that's what Ski should have. Surely she could manage. . . .

"Oh, Mike." She crumpled against him, and he held her tight. Long fingers smoothed over her rumpled hair as he whispered soothing sounds.

It was comfortable there in his arms; it felt good to be sympathized with instead of criticized. It was soothing to feel the strength in the arms around her. With a valiant effort, she pulled away from the safety he represented, and moved slowly toward her bedroom, looking back from the door.

She smiled and slid her tongue over the uneven front tooth. Mike grinned at the unconscious move and said, "Pick you up at eight?"

She nodded. "Thanks, Mike." She waited until the door closed behind him before she went to see if she'd live through the pain she knew would come from water beating on her bruised body and spirit.

At seven-thirty she was as ready as she'd ever be, having soaked herself in a hot-as-she-could-stand bath, loaded with baby oil, following that with a luke-warm shower, ending with a cold stinging spray that finally awakened her.

Surely Ski's homecoming would be informal, but she decided against jeans and took a red dress from the closet. She pulled it over her head, zipping the back as high as she could, then reaching over her shoulder to complete the closure. It fit closely to her waist and flared in a full circle just below her knees. A wide red belt, cinched tightly, made her small waist seem even smaller. Red patent pumps, a web of thin straps, gave her three more inches of height. She accented the outfit with red earrings, then finally reached for her cologne, spraying lightly around her throat.

When the door bell rang, her legs were trembling only slightly, and she was able to walk a fairly straight line. She pulled the door open to smile at Mike, standing tall in faded jeans and white knit shirt, open at the neck to show an expanse of tanned skin. His dark hair was brushed back, but a thick lock dropped over his forehead, showing a lot of silver.

"Come in, Mike," she said, stepping aside.

He grinned as he leaned against the door frame. "You survived."

"Barely," she said. "I may yet succumb."

"Not a chance. You look terrific." He straightened away from the door. "Let's go welcome Ski home."

She sat quietly while Mike drove and straightened as he pulled to the curb and stopped. "Is it a big party?" she asked.

"Uh-unh. Policemen have very few close friends, Joy." She looked hard at him. His voice was light, but she couldn't read the expression in his face as he came around to open the door for her. She stared uncertainly up into his face until he tugged on her arm, and she slid out to stand beside him.

"You won't be entirely among strangers, Joy. Maude and Paula are here."

"Oh," she said, remembering her curiosity about Paula and Mike. Was Paula the jealous type? "I haven't met Maude, but I've sampled her very delicious Christmas cookies."

He grinned. "That's right. She's also supplying the teriyaki meatballs tonight. Sorenson is supplying the pizza." He rolled his eyes, and she laughed. Her head hurt only a little bit.

They walked up an outside flight of stairs, and Mike knocked on a door marked "2A." It opened immediately, and they were pulled into what obviously was the living room, with couch and chairs pushed to the walls and about a dozen people sitting on the floor. Soft music, strictly easy listening, came from hidden speakers.

She looked at Mike, eyebrows peaked in surprise. He shrugged. "I forgot to tell you it's a party for the older generation."

"Joy," Ski said, coming toward them from the kitchen, where she could hear laughter.

"Hello, Ski. Nice to see you home." His left arm was in a sling, and a wide scratch along his chin was covered by a dark brown crust. He stopped in front of them, grinned at Mike, and kissed Joy's cheek.

"Meet everyone," he said, waving in the general direction of the group. "You know Paula." Paula saluted. He pointed. "Her sister, Maude."

Maude was a good bit older than Paula, pleasingly plump and with a ready smile just like Paula's. As they moved into the room, she met the others, most of whom were fellow policemen, some husband-and-wife teams among them.

"What are you drinking?" Mike asked.

"Either Coke or water, whichever has the least kick in it."

He squeezed her arm. "I'll see what I can do."

Ski and Paula came to her side, and she listened to their friendly teasing, answering a question when directed her way. She gathered enough information to decide it was Paula and Ski who dated, rather than Paula and Mike. And was surprised at the pleasure that simple knowledge brought her.

Mike returned, handing her a brandy glass filled with bubbly liquid. He leaned down and whispered, "Perrier. Guaranteed to bring you back to life."

She looked at the glass and said, "If that's true, I'll never be without it again, though I've been told it's only expensive H-two-O."

He laughed. "You may be right, but it's worth a try."

"Yes, it is," she agreed and sipped the icy liquid. There was only a bright, fresh taste, not really any flavor, but it went down her parched throat, bringing some welcome relief.

Listening to several conversations, she was surprised that none of them related to jobs. The party was to celebrate Ski's coming home from the hospital, recovering from a wound received in the line of duty. It seemed improbable that they wouldn't even mention it.

She said as much to Mike as she stood beside him

much later, the two of them alone for the first time.

"Doesn't anyone congratulate Ski on being able to come home? And don't they recognize you as the one who saved his life?"

"No." Her head swiveled around at the harshness of his voice, and she stared into steely gray eyes. "We don't talk about it because we all get physical check-ups next week, and we don't want anyone showing up with high blood pressure."

"I don't understand," she said.

"The man we stopped, the man who shot Ski, has arranged to plea-bargain. He'll be out on the streets again in a few years."

He stared at the glass in his hand and took a drink from it before going on. "So it isn't really a celebration, Joy, it's just a sort of regrouping to convince ourselves it's worth it to protect our honest citizens day after day against the same rotten system." His smile stretched his lips over white teeth that were ground together.

"Why do you stay?" she asked.

He looked her over. The heavy black hair, swinging on her shoulders; blue eyes wide and questioning; full lower lip shiny from her drink.

"You, Joy," he said softly. "For you, for Penny, for Ken." She looked down at her glass. "Yes," he added, "even for the enemy."

"It's a party, not a wake," Ski said, coming by and grinning at Joy. Paula stood near him, smiling. "Are you two arguing?" Before either could answer, he went on, "I haven't even had a chance to tell Joy how lovely she looks. Must admit red is more becoming than black." He turned to Paula. "The first time I saw her, it was almost Christmas, and she had on a black outfit with a—I don't know—sort of orchid-colored coat. She was lying on a dirty sidewalk with her hair full of snow."

"I knew she was a pickup," Paula said, smiling at Joy. "You never told me any details except that Mike tried to arrest her for DWI."

Mike grimaced. "Don't remind me. I'm still paying penance."

Joy listened to the light kidding and suddenly she felt part of their crowd, and she smiled at Paula, displaying her dimples, her tongue briefly touching the crooked tooth. She didn't remember feeling as though she belonged to anyone before—not even Ken. That had been the missing element in their marriage—she had never belonged. She didn't realize that the smile had faded from her lips and a strange awareness in her eyes had replaced it. She turned to Mike, and her glance locked with his for an instant, then went on around the room.

"Are you ready to leave?" he asked.

"Yes." Her voice had no expression, but when they said their good-byes, she told Ski, "I like your outfit better than Wilshire's, too."

He grinned. "I get the message and will stay out of the direct line of fire. I promise."

Beside her, Mike stiffened, but he put his hand beneath her elbow and guided her to the front door through the clusters of people lounging in various groups and positions. They called out good night as they left.

Outside, they stood by Mike's car, neither speaking as they gazed over the lights of the city, then up at the sky, full of twinkling lights not so bright as the earthly ones. But clear. There seemed to be no clouds or pollution between them and the millions of distant stars.

"How do you feel?"

Joy turned to look at him. "Must have been the glorified H-two-O. I feel great." As he opened the door for her, she added, "Or perhaps it was the company."

He smiled then. "Perhaps." He closed the door and went around to get in the driver's seat.

She leaned her head back on the seat and closed her eyes, paying little attention to the direction he took going to her apartment. She had managed a small slice of Sorenson's pizza, and her stomach was no longer queasy. She hadn't tried the meatballs for fear of stirring her delicate senses too much, but everyone else had enjoyed them. She had noticed that Mike stayed away from the pizza.

The car stopped, and she sat up to see they were in front of her apartment. Mike came around to open her door, standing aside as she slid from the seat.

"Do you make good coffee?" he asked.

"Best in the county," she claimed.

"I prefer to make my own judgment," he said, smiling down at her.

She nodded, taking her apartment key from her bag and handing it to him as they approached her door. The door swung open to a dimly lit room where she had left a light burning, a habit she had formed lately because she hated returning to a dark apartment alone.

"It'll only take a few minutes," she told him, walking quickly into the small kitchen area. He followed, leaning against the counter to watch her.

She reached into the cabinet for two mugs and then put the cream and sugar on the small table. When the perking stopped, she poured coffee into the mugs, and he took both of them to the table as she took spoons from a drawer.

"Just cream to color," she said.

He added cream to hers and stirred it, pushing it across the table as she sat down. They drank the coffee in silence until she looked up to meet his steady gaze.

"What now, Joy?" he asked.

She shrugged her shoulders. "Go on living the way someone does who has become accustomed to one way and must change."

"You never answered my question, you know."

"What?"

"Do you still love Ken? I realize that's an abstract question right now, but you've had time to analyze your feelings."

She studied the murky liquid in front of her. She'd waged a two-year battle for Ken's love with no help from the gallery. Because she didn't know it was a losing battle, and because she so much wanted to save her marriage, she'd never given up until the very last minute when, in desperation, she'd moved out of the house they shared. At first she thought he'd come after her and they could work out their problems. Ken had come after her and would have been happy for them to try again, but only if Joy could make civilized adjustments in her way of living.

So it had been Ken who, finally, snuffed out the love she'd wanted to last. She had done nothing except watch the flame grow dimmer and dimmer until it died a natural death.

She looked up, her eyes narrowed against the realization that she no longer had to cope with the love Ken had never appreciated. "No," she said slowly. "No, I don't love him."

"Then why did you go to pieces like that?"

Policemen need strong women; Mike was telling her she didn't qualify. Mike didn't know her very well, but she couldn't blame him for his opinion, not after the show she'd put on last night and this morning.

Her voice was slow in forming the words. "I suppose it was reaction." She shrugged. "Or perhaps I really was celebrating." She looked up and smiled at him. "Who knows?" She laughed softly. "But I found out one thing." Dimples flashed with her quick grin.

"What's that?"

"I'd never make an alcoholic. There must be nicer ways to torture oneself."

"Or to celebrate." He got up to pour them more coffee and was smiling as he leaned over her. "You're right. You do make good coffee." He brushed his lips over the top of her head before he walked back to sit opposite her. "Tomorrow is the first Sunday I've been off in months. Would you like to drive over to Lake Tahoe?"

The invitation came as a surprise, and she didn't answer immediately. His eyebrows climbed. "It's only a Sunday excursion to see how the other half lives, Joy."

She laughed. "Tahoe is certainly different from what I'm used to. I'd love to go. Conan's has a building dedication there, and we're supposed to go to the open house next month. I'd love to get a sneak preview."

"We could leave around nine and have breakfast out somewhere if you like."

"All right."

He stood up and stretched. "Thanks for the coffee. That should keep me awake till I get home."

Joy walked Mike to the door in stocking feet, since she had long since discarded the frivolous sandals. Without them, she had a long way to look up to see Mike's expression, and even then, she couldn't read any of his thoughts behind eyes half-closed as he looked down at her.

At the door, Mike turned her to face him, slipping his arms around her to lift her against him, lowering his head to place his mouth on hers, gently at first, but as she moved her head to protest, his lips became insistent, forcing hers apart. Then she was free, staring into the darkness of his eyes.

"About nine?" he asked quietly.

Her voice barely audible over the pressure in her chest, she answered, "Yes."

Chapter Nine

The hangover from the day before persisted even though she hadn't tasted alcohol at Ski's party. Her eyelids were swollen and sore, and she had trouble opening them wide enough to find her way into the bathroom.

With coffee perking, she went to look for something suitable to wear and came across a violet-blue sweater and slightly darker blue pants with matching jacket. Navy walking shoes and shoulder bag completed the outfit, and she fastened a matching band around her hair just as the door bell rang.

The light was behind Mike as she opened the door. His face was shadowed, but she smiled up at him and stepped aside as he moved through the doorway.

Smiling, he brushed the top of her head with his mouth and sniffed. "More 'best in the county' coffee?"

"Yes. Would you like some?"

"I was hoping you'd ask." He followed her into the kitchen and sat down as she placed two coffees on the table. "You mentioned once that you preferred hot chocolate."

She remembered. "Sometimes when it's very cold, but early mornings demand coffee."

"I agree," he said. "Hangover gone?" he asked, smiling across at her.

She laughed. "I can shake my head now and not be afraid it will drop off." She shook her head to prove it and added, "Never again."

"That's a long time," he said.

"I learn quickly," she said, looking into her coffee cup. "Whatever the problem might be, the alcohol blackout is very temporary."

"Suppose we declare today to be up-and-at-'em day—no dark thoughts, no regrets, just plain old glad-to-be-alive-and-together day. What say?"

"I say bravo, bravo, double for both of us," she said, laughing.

"Consider it done," he said, standing to take both cups to the sink and turning to look over his shoulder. "By the way, the temperature is much lower than yesterday. Take a heavier jacket in case that suit isn't warm enough later in the evening."

"Okay." The lavender all-weather coat, with the winter lining still zipped into it, was the first thing she saw, and she removed it from the hanger to throw it over her arm. She preceded him out the door, and they linked arms to walk to his car parked at the curb. The wind had picked up and blew strong out of the northwest.

She shivered. "I'm ready for spring," she said.

"Where did this weather come from?" She hadn't listened to the news or taken her usual walk down the street for a Sunday paper.

Mike pulled the car from the curb, guiding it expertly through deserted back streets toward the interstate that would take them into South Lake Tahoe.

They had been driving several minutes when he said, "We're about an hour from Minden, where there's a place that serves a great breakfast."

"I didn't know Minden had enough people to support a restaurant."

He laughed. "It isn't exactly a restaurant, just a place that has good food. Actually it's a private home. I think you'll like it, but you take pot luck. Whatever Grace has is what's on the menu. Always good."

"In an hour I won't be too choosy," she told him.

"Look," he said and pointed to their right as they topped a steep incline and started the winding curves downward. The line of hills several miles away were almost hidden behind a curtain of white as snow blew southward.

"How pretty," she said, staring at the scene. Snow in their area in late April wasn't the rule, but it had happened many times, usually only a few inches that was gone in a short while. There were few clouds, but a line of dark gray followed the horizon.

"The ski stragglers will be happy to see that," she said.

"I doubt this will help them much."

Traffic was heavy, and she wondered idly where everyone was going in such a hurry. Head resting on the back of the car seat, she decided she was glad to be with Mike going wherever he chose. For one day, there was no place she had to be—no deadlines to meet, no decisions to make. It was all up to Mike.

The whir of the windshield wipers startled her and she sat up. The snow had reached them. She turned her head to meet Mike's smiling glance.

"We may not get any farther than breakfast," he told her.

He slowed to follow the exit sign and made a left turn under the interstate for a quarter mile before he turned into the yard of a small green clapboard cottage. Three cars were there ahead of them, and a big semitrailer, motor running, was parked alongside the curb.

The snow fell steadily as they got out of the car, and they ran through it to the door. Inside, the lights were on, and the room they walked into was bright and cheerful. Booths lined the wall of what was once a large living room, and three tables were well spaced at angles in the center. Mike led her to a booth past a family of four at a table and a couple sitting close together in a booth. A man, apparently through with his meal, stood by the cash register, his attention on the wide windows where the snow was beginning to blow past in misty white sheets.

Joy looked at the menu, printed on three-hole notebook paper, lying on a paper placemat. The only item was the Sunday morning special, which looked as if it had been made up for hungry loggers.

"Well, Mike, no wonder it's snowing. Where have you been?"

Joy looked up at the woman who had spoken as she poured coffee into cups already on the table and placed the pot where they could reach it. Her smile stretched wide in her rounded face, and there was a warm gleam in the faded hazel eyes.

Mike stood up and gathered the plump figure into his arms and looked down at her, smiling. "Busy, Grace. You know how it is." He turned to Joy. "This is Joy Strayer. We were on our way to Lake Tahoe, but from the looks of the weather, you may have to feed us dinner, too."

"No problem," Grace said after greeting Joy. She looked back at Mike. "I read about you and Ski. Are both of you all right?"

"Yes. Ski's already back chasing girls, and he'll be back to full duty in ten days or so."

She clucked her tongue. "I worry, Mike. There's mean people out there."

"According to the courts that free them, Grace, they're innocent and only break the law because we drive them to it."

Joy's eyes fastened on Mike's face as he spoke, his voice showing no emotion, and she decided she wouldn't like to be on the receiving end of the cold anger she saw in his gray eyes.

Still shaking her head, Grace said, "Fresh biscuits ready in five minutes. You want the full fare?" Her eyes went over Joy in a manner suggesting she couldn't handle the big meal.

"Joy?" Mike asked.

"I'm starved," she said. "I'm not sure I can wait five minutes."

"I'll be right back," Grace said, moving quickly across the room, taking orders and making friendly comments. She returned to their booth almost immediately with a trio of jams and jellies and was off on the run again.

A small silence fell between them, and, Joy, her thoughts skipping between a small worry about the weather and the man across from her, paid little attention until Mike spoke.

"I stopped by Conan's while you were in Red Lodge. Did Tom mention it?"

Her head came up in surprise. "No. But then, I've only talked to him on the phone. What were you doing over there?"

"Investigating a robbery down the street at a branch bank. One of the ladies who cleans your building early in the morning saw the car, and I went to ask for her address. All we had was the street name, no number."

"What was Tom doing at work so early?"

"He was grumbling something about his marketing consultant being out of town and that he didn't know where some figures were kept."

"Nonsense," she said, shaking her head. "Tom Conan knows where to find every program I've ever run on every project I've handled the past five years since I've been in that position."

He laughed, and Joy felt a pleasant sensation sweep

across her nerve center. The smile lit the darkness of the gray eyes and lifted the corners of the wide mouth. He leaned his elbows on the table, studying her.

"I told him I'd met you, informally, and he started talking about you like a favorite daughter. Is that how you came by such an impressive job, being a relative?"

Mike watched her eyes narrow and was unprepared for the hardness of her voice as she told him, "I'm no one's relative, Mike. Tom hired me from the Distributive Education class when I was a senior in high school." She looked away from him, focusing for a moment on the remembered feelings she'd had as Tom interviewed her.

"You must have had some qualifications or he wouldn't have considered you."

"He hired me as a trainee. I worked myself up from there." She met his glance then and smiled, two dimples chasing elusively along her cheeks. "I guess after he spent all that money breaking me into the outfit, he thought he ought to keep me to recoup his investment."

"From what he told me, he's positive of that."

"Why?"

"Why what?"

"Why were you discussing me?"

"I was interested," Mike said. "And Tom enjoyed answering my questions. After a couple of minutes, I didn't even have to ask. He told me you were his marketing analyst and consultant and that you trav-

eled extensively throughout the Western states to
scout projects; that your figures were the basis with
which he started original bids on million-dollar deals.
Anything from bridges to dams to fifty-story buildings.''

She was staring at him as he talked, his long fingers
pushing a fork back and forth beside his coffee cup.
He looked up to meet her curious expression.

"Are you sure you're not a relative? You're too
pretty to know how to handle all that stuff." He
grinned, shaking his head, and sat back in the booth
as their breakfast was placed in front of them.

"Good heavens," Joy whispered. "Are we supposed to eat all of this?"

"Absolutely," he whispered back. "Grace gets
positively hostile if you leave so much as a crumb on
your plate."

She forgot Mike's halfway teasing questions about
her job and dug into the ham, pan-fried potatoes, per-
fectly formed sunny-side up eggs and fresh-from-the-
oven biscuits.

"Does being angry give you an appetite?"

She looked up, a forkful of food poised near her
mouth. "Being angry?"

He was still teasing. "Yes, you were getting your
dander up when I indicated you got your prestigious
job by being a relative rather than on qualifications."

She nodded. "I do resent it if people believe as you
do. You're certainly not the first. But mostly I ignore
ill manners." She grinned to take the sting from her
words. "To answer your question, though. I don't

need anything to give me an appetite. I manage quite well."

Grace came by with another pot of coffee, and Mike turned his attention once more to the windows and the weather. "Heard anything about the storm recently?"

"They said it's worse south of us. It's only supposed to be a couple of inches or so around us."

"Enough to cause the highway patrols some trouble," Mike said.

She nodded as she moved away. "Call if you need anything."

"I hate to be a pessimist," Joy told him, looking out the front door as a couple came in. "But it's going to have to slow down if we're to get only two inches. This is the way it snows when we get a foot or so." She recalled the deepest snow of the season, the one when she lost the baby and met Mike, months ago or a lifetime, depending on whose point of view.

Mike laughed. "Eat your breakfast and don't worry."

Doing as she was told, she scooped up the last forkful of potatoes, leaned back and sighed, wiping her mouth with her napkin. "You didn't exaggerate the goodness or the amount," she said, smiling, and the twin dimples flashed impishly, much the way they'd done on Friday night when she tangled with the cognac and came out second-best. The dimples fascinated him—that and the tongue exercise over the front tooth.

They stood up and moved to the cash register, where Grace was talking to a truck driver who had finished his breakfast and was eyeing the snow. He shook his head.

"These late storms are murder. No one takes them seriously, and they drive like they do when it's eighty-five degrees." He accepted his change from Grace and stuck a toothpick in his mouth. "This is one time I wish I was headed north."

"You'll probably run out of it past Tahoe, Bert," Grace told him. "Just take it easy and watch out for the race drivers." She reached for Mike's ticket and called after the departing trucker, "See you on your way back next Saturday." Bert waved and walked across the street to the big diesel semi, climbed behind the wheel, and pulled into the access road that would take him onto the southbound lane of the highway. Joy watched the clumsy-looking vehicle gather speed, its side proclaiming Flammable Liquids. Smoke billowed from the diesel pipes behind the cab as the semi disappeared over the hill. She walked outside with Mike and they stood, side by side, gazing at the winter wonderland around them.

"Shall we?" he asked, looking down into her up-turned face. Snow clung to her hair and tangled on her eyelashes, and she laughed, eyes sparkling with excitement much like a child with her first sled. He reached for her hand, wanting suddenly to pick her up and hold her close to him, wanting to taste the snowflakes that settled on her mouth. As Joy licked at the snowflakes his body tightened at the pure sexiness of the move.

Pushing away the erring thoughts, he pulled her

with him, and they raced to the car, skidding as they stopped on the passenger side. He opened the door, brushing her hair and jacket as he helped her inside. When he slid beneath the wheel, his hair was covered with snow, camouflaging the gray.

"Christmas in April," he said, staring through the coated windshield as he started the car and switched on the wipers. He let the engine run for a minute to warm, and she glanced at him now as he concentrated on getting them back on the interstate.

"It's getting worse," he said, looking at the thick curtain around them. "I think we'd better get off at the next exit and go back while we can." They had gone perhaps half a mile and the next exit was some miles ahead of them. He gave her a brief smile. "Wouldn't you know that if nothing else could ruin our day, Mother Nature would try her luck?"

She was watching his mouth, the way it curved as he smiled, and for a moment felt it on hers when he had kissed her that night long ago when she had stayed in his apartment. He'd kissed her lightly since then, but that was the kiss that stayed in her memory, when they talked about being afraid of life and circumstances. She corrected herself; when they talked about Joy being afraid.

But Mike had his doubts, too, she remembered. A giant-sized he-man policeman, afraid of loving too well, but afraid of nothing else in this world. He'd been gentle with her, even though she sensed disapproval of her attitude. Mike could be gentle or hard as nails, but he didn't want to get involved with a woman

YOURS FREE

4 Harlequin American Romances™
and a fashion tote

It's our way of introducing you to our Harlequin Reader Service that's so much easier and less expensive than buying your novels retail.

As a subscriber, you'll receive 4 new books to preview every month. Always before they're available in stores. Always for the same low price. Always with the right to return the shipment and owe nothing.

AR2TMU

►►► FREE BOOKS & TOTE BAG ►►►

who readily admitted she needed love in a world where the real thing was hard to come by.

She shivered and turned to look out the windows of the car, frosted into opaque white, the defroster and wipers doing very little to help.

Mike leaned forward over the wheel, frowning into the blinding curtain that descended, obscuring everything, including the road. For the first time, she began to feel uneasy about their predicament, and she looked back at Mike as he made an exclamation.

A small car hurtled past them, leaving inches between the two vehicles, skidding sideways out of their path as Mike pumped lightly on his brakes. A moment later, the car was gone, disappearing into the white wall ahead of them.

"Idiot," Mike said through clenched teeth.

Joy sat stiffly beside him, realizing the other car had missed them by inches, with Mike's skillful handling of the braking of his car the only thing that had prevented a crash. Their progress was inch by inch now, and the dark wall to her right was only an outline through the snow as the car rolled to a stop. She looked at Mike, who was staring at the same darkness she had seen. At the same time, they realized what it was. The truck that had pulled out of Grace's lot lay on its side, half on the road.

"Stay in the car," Mike ordered, opening the door to step out into the blowing snow. In a moment all she could see of him was a shadowy outline. Rolling down the window, she blinked as the icy wind whipped snow into her face.

"Mike," she called, but her voice was thrown back into the car. She opened the door and stepped outside, her feet immediately sinking into the accumulation of snow that had drifted onto the roadbed.

As she struggled toward the outline of the truck, Mike came to meet her. His hand on her arm to hold her steady, he yelled, "The cab is hanging partly off the road, and the driver's trapped. I'm going to try to get up there and get him out, and maybe I can use the CB and call for help." She couldn't see anything but his mouth, shaping words she strained to hear. "Can you drive the car along the side of the truck so I can climb on top of it and get into the cab?"

She nodded, turning back to the car. His hand on her arm stopped her, and she looked up as he bent to speak again. "Be careful, Joy. Don't use the brake if you can help it, and don't get too close to the drop-off. Stay close alongside the truck."

Nodding again, she struggled to get back into the car, leaving the window down to stick her head out in order to see better. It was a losing game; she still couldn't see. Watching Mike climb on the hood of the car, she eased into low gear for slow, heavy pulling and inched forward. Mike's arms signaled she was close enough and she held her breath as he caught hold of the truck door. Snow had already frozen it shut, and he pounded on it, trying to loosen it enough to allow it to open. Her breath released when she saw the door come open and Mike swing it back to lean into the cab. A few heart-beats later, he backed away, looking toward her, and she stuck her head out the window to hear him.

Cupping one hand to his mouth, he yelled, "I need something to slide under him to pull with. See if there's a towel in the back."

Leaning over the backseat, she searched for anything that could help, spotting the coat she had thrown in when Mike said it was supposed to turn colder. That was a masterpiece of understatement, as they were finding out. She took the coat and backed out into the snow, moving step by slippery step to get close enough to hand it to Mike.

His hands contacted hers, and he recognized the item he held. "He's bleeding, Joy," he said, hesitating.

"It doesn't matter. Use it." It was time the coat was replaced anyway.

Without a word, he turned back to the truck and the man inside. She waited, thinking she might be able to help him lift the man out of the truck cab.

"I can't get him loose," Mike said, desperation edging his voice.

Stepping to the front of the car, Joy found the bumper with her bare hands, fingers becoming numb almost immediately. Holding to the hood ornament she found by feeling along the grill, she pulled herself up, catching one of Mike's legs to hoist herself. She felt him twist to look down at her, but she couldn't hear a word he said as the snow caught his voice, blurring it. When she stood upright, she was able to brace against the open door and stared, shocked, at the face of the driver who had paid for his breakfast just ahead of them at Grace's place. A trickle of blood ran over his chin, and his face was pasty white. She looked at Mike, frustration tightening his mouth.

"If I crawl over in back of him, maybe I can free his legs, Mike," she said.

"No. This thing could go over that bank any minute."

"Then what?" she asked.

He looked at the man and back at her and nodded. His eyes held hers an instant before he said tersely, "Hurry."

Her numb feet were clumsy as she felt for a footing behind the tilted driver's seat. Inside the cab she brushed the snow from her eyes and was able to see exactly what they faced. The driver slumped over the wheel, long arms dangling over the seat. As she crouched half on the seat and half on the floor, she saw his leg caught between the heavy gear shift and the steering column, which had crumpled like a toy. Her breath was ragged as she looked up into Mike's face, way up from her, peering in the door above the man.

"Do you have a knife?" she asked.

As she waited for him to work his hands into his pocket, she untied the heavy laces on the man's boots. She gasped as a sudden blast of wind shook the truck and it moved. Clumsy fingers refused to work to remove the boots, and she gave up as she heard Mike's voice.

"Joy," he called, and she reached upward to take the knife, already opened, from his hand. Trying not to feel the vibration of the truck beneath them, she

clenched her teeth and sawed at the heavy pants material with the knife. Once she punctured it, the knife
cut sharply and she went around the pant leg just at
the knee. Now all she had to do was remove the boot
and his leg would be free.

She raised her head. "Can you pull him up just a
little, Mike?"

He didn't answer, but she saw him reach under the
thick shoulders and the leg she was watching moved a
little. The man groaned, and she bit her lip. If her
fingers weren't so useless, she thought, and flexed
them several times trying to limber them up a little.
She bent back to the laces, pulling them completely
out of the boot. Prying the heavy leather apart, she
caught the boot and tugged, gritting her teeth when
the man groaned again. Her body was bathed in cold
sweat, and she was freezing, her muscles screaming in
protest as she yanked on the boot, falling sideways as
it came off in her hand.

"Now, Mike," she called and slumped on the seat
as the body beside her moved slowly upward.

Hidden from her view, Mike struggled with his
limp burden, and she stared at the CB equipment dangling near her. She had no idea how to use it and
blinked her eyes to read the instructions in fine print
on the microphone. Fingers barely working, she removed the mike from the hook where it rested and
pushed the button that instructed Send and couldn't
remember what should be said in an emergency situa-
tion.

The only word she could think of was "mayday,"

which she repeated into the mike she held. Not knowing if she was getting through the crackling wires, she repeated "mayday" and gave instructions as best she could.

"Emergency. Accident with injuries near first exit on Interstate Highway 395 south of Minden. Mayday. Mayday."

"Joy," Mike yelled at her from the open door. "Get out of there; this thing's shaky." Long arms reached to pull her up, and she depended on his strength to get her out because her arms and legs no longer functioned on their own. Hours later, it seemed, she was yanked through the door, and they both slid off the hood of Mike's car. He had somehow gotten the man into the backseat, covered with her coat and Mike's jacket. They shivered so hard their bodies jerked. He shoved her into the seat and crawled in beside her.

"Did the CB work?" he asked, struggling for breath.

She half lay in the seat. "I don't know." Her teeth chattered, and she clamped them together. "I've never used one before."

He leaned over the wheel, eyes closed for a moment, before he straightened. Without another word, he started the car and adjusted the defroster to full blast, leaving his window down to stick his head out as he backed away from the big truck hanging over the embankment. He could no longer see the road and had no idea how far he could go backward before going over the bank on the opposite side of the road.

The car slid and the wheels spun as he tried to move forward, succeeding only a little before it stalled.

"I'd better just wait and let the car warm up so he can thaw out," he said as he turned to look at her. His gaze softened as he took in the black hair plastered to her face, her jacket soaked and clinging to her shivering body. "If you got through, someone should find us soon." Straining to see through the windshield, he added, "Not much of a day off for you."

"B-Bert isn't having s-such a g-good day, either," she chattered.

"Bert?"

"That's what Grace called him when he checked out at breakfast."

He looked over at her. "I didn't even notice."

She managed a grin. "Not very policemanlike, w-would you s-say?"

He shook his head. "You're right. Not observant at all." He wasn't about to tell her he'd been watching the cloud of black hair swing on her shoulders and blue eyes dancing as she watched the first of the dangerous snowfall before they ventured into it.

"What happened to all the traffic we saw earlier? Surely some of them got through, or it's a hell of a lot worse farther south." Mike's voice took on a grim tone, and the fright that had been threatening her took over as she realized they were far from out of danger.

Bert groaned and both of them looked over the backseat as he began to shiver and tried to sit up. Joy stretched upward and leaned across the seat to put her hands on his chest.

"No," she said, her voice firm as she caught a thrashing arm, pushing with what little strength she had to get it back under her coat. She looked back at Mike as he made an exclamation.

"Thank God," he said.

"What?"

"I think it's a snowplow or tractor of some kind." He opened the door and stepped out into a knee-deep drift of snow. She couldn't follow where he was going but suddenly saw the big vehicle as it loomed in the road near the truck. She hadn't heard a thing. She was still holding on to Bert's arms when the door on her side of the car opened and a big form appeared, arctic wear shrouding any appearance of a human being.

"You all right, ma'am?" a muffled voice inquired.

She managed a grin. "I'm much better now that I know there's someone else in the world." Sliding down on the wet car seat, she said, "Bert's the one who needs attention."

The figure disappeared from sight, and she saw him struggle with the frozen handle on the back door, wrenching it open to let in a swirl of snow. He backed out again, yelling at someone she didn't see.

Twisting in the seat as she sensed movement around her, Joy jumped as Mike jerked the door open on the driver's side and fell into the seat, breathing hard.

"They say there are several bad accidents south of us, and no one can get through except the snowplows. These guys say it's the worst storm they've ever seen in these parts after January, and it took them some time to get started with the equipment." He reached for her. "Joy," he said, pulling her to his icy chest. "You'll probably catch your death of cold from this little outing."

Shivering, she sat quietly within the circle of his arms, not bothering to move when a man tapped on Mike's window, and he rolled it down to talk to him.

After a moment, Mike said, "They're going to take us in on the plow. Can you walk?"

In the struggle to get to the heavy vehicle, she concentrated on staying upright with Mike's help and refused to let herself think what could have happened to them. She would let her fright catch up with her sometime in the future.

Chapter Ten

Vaguely aware of what went on around her, Joy half slept, wrapped in a blanket in the emergency room of Wilshire General Hospital, where the rescue team had left the three of them. She didn't know where Mike was or the condition of the man they had tried to rescue. Listening to the half-audible conversation of two nurses nearby, she knew they weren't the only ones who'd been stranded in the freak late-spring storm.

"Joy?"

Her eyes flew open at the sound of Mike's voice, and she sat up. "I was wondering if you had abandoned me."

He grinned. "You do look like something that's been thrown away." He sat next to her. "Bert's being taken care of, but I'm afraid we ruined your coat. Besides the blood, we ripped it down the back."

"Small loss," she told him. "As long as we survived." It had served its purpose in warming Bert as long as he needed it.

"I called Ski," Mike said. "He'll be over as soon as

he can." He looked over her blanket-wrapped form. "I'm afraid your clothing is pretty much the worse for wear, too." He grinned. "It's much warmer here, but not exactly streaking weather. How're we gonna get you home?"

She looked down at the olive drab of the hospital blanket she clutched around her. "Maybe I can borrow this and play heap big Injun squaw till I can get me some clothes." A quick smile brought the twin dimples into view briefly as she regarded him. He still wore the sport slacks and shirt he'd started out with, wrinkled and only slightly damp now.

"Was your jacket ruined, too?" she asked.

"Yes." He leaned back in the chair, still watching the play of expressions across Joy's face. "This will teach me not to ask for a Sunday off. I get into less trouble on duty."

She was silent, thinking of the weekend that resulted in their close brush with death following so closely behind Ski's hospitalization in this same hospital.

The outside door to the emergency room opened, and they looked up as Ski came hurrying in. He stood looking down at them, his hand on his hip.

"Can't leave you two alone even one day without you getting into trouble." He touched Joy's shoulder. "Latest fashion for Tahoe?"

Mike stood up, and Ski's glance moved over his big frame in untidy sports clothes. "We tangled with unfriendly forces, Ski, and we need some tender loving care, not your smart remarks. Take us to Joy's apartment so she can get into something a little more appropriate for Sunday afternoon."

"Where's your car?" Ski asked, still smiling at Joy's informal attire.

"I finally killed that old battery by spinning ourselves into a no-win war with mud and snow, plus leaving the lights on while we were trying our rescue tactics. It's been towed to the headquarters service area for rejuvenation."

"It was a foregone conclusion it would happen sooner or later." Ski looked at Joy. "At least he didn't pull that old story of running out of gas to have you to himself. I must admit a rescue in a snowstorm is quite original."

Mike shook his head at Ski's teasing comments and left the two of them to go to the desk. Joy watched him talking, using his hands to demonstrate, and smiling at the young nurses there who immediately were captivated by his dark good looks.

He came back toward them and said, "Okay, Joy, you're cleared to wear your sarong home. I promised to return it next week."

Ski led the way out to his car, where Paula had kept the motor running to keep it warm. As Joy and Mike slid into the backseat, Ski asked, "Are you going to tell us what happened?"

Paula smiled at Ski's questions, glancing over her shoulder as she drove slowly away from the hospital, but her sympathetic glance met Joy's in the mirror as Mike talked.

Briefly he described their harrowing experience, his

mouth settling into a grim line as he said, "Some idiot in a sports car was racing up that road, and I assume Bert jackknifed to avoid hitting him. He almost got us, too."

Joy remembered the small car that came at them, missing by inches, and she turned to look at Mike. "How do you know that's what caused Bert's trouble?"

"He told me." Mike gave her a small grin. "The language he used in describing what happened would melt all the snow we saw." He looked around them at the bright late-afternoon sunshine and shook his head. "Can you believe ten inches of snow on April twenty-eighth a few miles from here and not even a flake in Reno?"

"No," she said and did find it hard to believe even after being there.

Paula followed her directions and a few minutes later pulled up at her apartment house. Mike smiled down at her. "What will the neighbors think about your costume?"

"My neighbors don't see me enough not to think it's the way I always dress. All I need is for you two to be in uniform bringing me home, and I could really start some gossip." She slid out of the car to stand beside Mike, looking at the two in the front seat. "Thanks for the rescue. I'll be by to see you sometime during the week, Paula."

Mike walked with her to the door, took her key and unlocked it. "Will you be all right if I leave you now?" he asked. "I need to check on my car while

I've got a ride by the station, to see if they've got it running again.''

"Sure, I'm fine—now," she told him, stressing the now.

He hesitated. "I'm sorry, Joy. You didn't even get lunch."

"It was a good breakfast, though. Maybe you should call Grace and tell her we made it back."

"I'm sure she heard about it over her CB." He touched her cheek. "I'll pick up the blanket sometime next week and return it to the hospital. Get some rest and I'll try to make this up to you another time."

"It's all right, Mike. I'm just glad it didn't turn out so badly after all."

"You're a good sport, Joy. See you." He lifted his hand and turned to leave her. She stood watching his wide shoulders stretching the wrinkled shirt, saw the hesitation in his stride and the shoulders swing back toward her. Her head was lifted, soft black hair dry now and escaping from the ribbon, curling against her cheek.

He stood as if uncertain for a moment, then he was back in front of her, looking down into wide eyes the color of the sky above Lake Tahoe in the spring. His hands went beneath her elbows, still wrapped in the blanket, only her hands visible as she clutched it around her. He propelled her into his arms, encircling blanket and all, holding her close with his cheek against the top of her head. Just for a moment. Slowly, using his chin, he pushed her head backward, moving quickly to claim her lips as they parted in surprise. She felt the sweep of his warm breath inside her mouth, the tip of his tongue slipping beneath hers, teasing around it, suddenly thrusting into her mouth as his arms tightened.

Somehow, one of his hands found its way beneath the blanket, cupping her hip, lifting her until her body rested against the hardness of his. The eroticism of knowing there was one layer of material between her bare flesh and Mike's obvious desire hit with a quivering arrow of stabbing hunger from within her own body.

Answering his demanding mouth, she gave him the tip of her tongue, only to have him take it all with his, wrapping it and tugging gently. The moan that came from deep in his chest echoed through her mouth, awakening an answering cry that spoke of her need for the love she'd been denied.

Entwined in his arms, Joy felt the sensuous movement as their bodies clamored for more of the intoxicating pleasures roused by their kisses. Mike's thigh pressed against her legs, pushing her back across the threshold, and the sound of the closing door barely touched her consciousness. With a quick movement, he swept the blanket downward and her naked breasts rested against his chest. With a gasp, he released her lips and let his eyes roam over the rounded firmness of the pale flesh, the rosy tips just visible.

"Joy." The whisper came from him with the same raw craving he'd awakened in her. He half lifted her as he lowered his mouth to take the hardened bud into his mouth, rolling his tongue around it to suck gently.

For an instant, she held the dark shaggy head to her, then she pushed at the wide shoulders she'd held tightly a moment before.

"Please, Mike."

Slowly he let her go, although his arms still held her close. His breath came in short, quick puffs, stirring the curling tendrils of hair in front of her ear, his lips touching the feathery tips of long eyelashes. He didn't look at her but, instead, pulled the blanket up to cover her shoulders and breasts. When finally their eyes met, his were dark and shadowed by lashes, and the lips that had sent her heart soaring were closed in a thin line.

The muscles in his throat moved convulsively before he spoke in a quiet voice. "I wanted that too much to deny myself, Joy. It was every bit what I thought it would be, and even though I should apologize..." He let his voice slide away and watched her expression without smiling.

"I—I..." It was her turn to swallow over the sudden lump in her throat. Mike hadn't really wanted to kiss her; he was just giving in to male curiosity. "Don't apologize, Mike." She shuffled her feet backward, holding on to the blanket. Somehow she didn't want his apology; she, too, had enjoyed the caresses. "Good night, Mike."

With an all-encompassing glance over her blanket-covered body, he said, "Good night, Joy," and closed the door behind him.

THE FIRST TIME HE HELD Joy Strayer in his arms he'd sensed she could be trouble for him. A tiny alarm of warning had sounded, a strange tingle through his body. With nothing to back up that feeling, he'd stared at the pale face of the young woman he held in his arms as he and Ski took her to the hospital emergency room. With a snowstorm paralyzing a good part of the city, and no ambulance available, they'd elected to take her in their patrol car when she fainted as he questioned her, confident she was driving under the influence of alcohol or drugs.

Now as he rode in the back of Paula's car, he stared out the window, knowing how right he'd been to think Joy meant trouble. He'd all but forgotten about her when he met her at the tennis courts, bought her a cup of hot chocolate, and took her home with him. And kissed her, wanting more, but he hadn't insisted, knowing the uncertainty she was feeling as she went through the traumatic experience of a divorce.

I should know, after all these years, to trust my instincts where women and criminals are concerned, he thought now. *I can't afford her; she's the kind of woman who'll want a policeman to give up the streets for a "safe" desk job. No woman wants a man she has to lose sleep over 365 days of the year for twenty years. If he lives long enough for retirement after twenty.* He had twelve years with the police force, and for those twelve years, he'd shunned women like Joy Strayer, women who needed to be protected from the hard, cold facts of life, especially the brutal facts of life for a policeman.

In spite of himself, his thoughts left the negative

side of his silent argument and went back to Joy Strayer, more or less wrapped in a loose blanket, a blanket that had slid away from her with surprising ease as his hands moved of their own accord to expose her body to his view. His body was suddenly rock hard as he once more relived the wildly abandoned kiss they shared, the view of her pale shoulders and the upward thrust of small but rounded breasts pushed into his chest, her open mouth accepting the demand of his.

"Are you okay?" Ski turned in the seat to glance over his shoulder, and Mike was aware he'd moaned as he felt again the hard rosy tip of her breast as he pulled it into his mouth.

He mumbled something to Ski that satisfied his partner. *My God,* he thought, *when you've made such a colossal error in judgment, what do you do for an encore?*

His friends in the motor pool at the police garage had worked hard on his car to have it running when Paula and Ski dropped him off. He accepted their friendly teasing about the snowplow rescue and went home.

With a big towel around him after a quick shower, he placed a call to his mother in Denver. She would have heard about the unseasonable weather and, from a policeman's widow's experience, would know it meant extra work for the force.

"Oh, Mike, I was just watching the news," Phyllis Gresham exclaimed as she recognized his voice. "Are you all right?"

"Sure, Mother, how about yourself? Any snow in

Denver yet?'' His voice was as carefree as it always was when he talked to Phyllis.

"We had a beautiful day. I went with the McCalls down to Colorado Springs to the air show, and we just got back half an hour ago. I didn't know the storm had hit so hard until a few minutes ago. Were you on duty?"

He laughed. "Would you believe I had today off, the first Sunday in I can't remember when?"

"Lucky you," his mother said, and he didn't bother to tell her he'd been caught in the snowstorm with a delectable armful of woman he wanted with a passion he couldn't remember ever feeling for any woman. He wanted her, but he couldn't have her. He had the feeling that once involved with Joy Strayer, he'd be stuck. A hard-hitting policeman like Mike Gresham was not suitable husband material for a gentle person such as Joy Strayer. And somehow he knew she'd be looking for a husband—not a casual affair.

Chapter Eleven

Monday—the start of a new week and a new life for her. Alone. As she moved quickly to dress, Joy's mind went over the weekend that had gone by in such a shadow, starting with the devastating blow of the divorce papers on Friday. Ski's coming-home party was an enjoyable break between her bout with the cognac and the aborted sight-seeing trip with Mike. She and Mike were safe, Bert would recover, and her life would go on without Ken and Penny. She had a good and demanding job—for that she was thankful.

Standing by the kitchen sink with a cup of coffee in her hand, she remembered Mike's kiss and her response, which had surprised her and probably had shocked him, especially in the light of her exhibition Friday night. A shimmer of warmth spread through her at the memory of their shared moment of passion. If she could feel that intensely for an almost-stranger, perhaps there was hope for her yet.

Still, it was a reluctant gaze that rested on the table where the letter from the lawyer still lay. The frightening finality of the action outlined in the innocent-looking piece of paper turned her stomach over, and she put the coffee cup in the sink and went back into the bedroom to find slippers to go with the cornflower-blue jumper and blue print blouse she had chosen for a busy Monday morning at the office. It brought out the deep color of her eyes and minimized the circles beneath them.

Resolutely she turned her thoughts to the Red Lodge project. It promised to be an all-consuming occupation for her in the weeks to come, and then she'd be able to keep up with it by occasional trips to the small town and by briefings with Tom Conan and the town council in Red Lodge. In the meantime she would concentrate on the fact that she was no longer a married woman, but a divorcée, however reluctant, and that she would have to learn to live with the uncertainty she felt a good bit of the time. Learn to live alone again—something she'd never wanted to do. Live without love. To herself she could admit how frightening that thought was, but to the world she could offer a serene countenance. With practice.

Against her better judgment, she thought of Mike. Brave and strong, the way policemen should be. The way he believed she should be. *Stand up for yourself, believe in yourself; show the world—and Ken—you can manage alone,* she imagined Mike telling her. She bit into her lip, confidence in herself, in being able to get through the weeks to come, at a dangerously low ebb.

Automatically following her daily routine, she drove the familiar route to Conan's, smiled hello to friendly co-workers and sat down in front of the familiar desk. The tasks took care of themselves as the hours passed, and after lunch, she transferred the bulky Red Lodge file from the cabinet to her desk and removed the ledgers she needed to work from at the computer terminal. Engrossed in the figures she was adjusting to fit the new construction costs, she looked up at Tom Conan as he stopped in front of her.

"The insurance adjusters will be here next week, Joy," he said, looking at the spread she was working on. "About Wednesday we should go talk to Mayor Sangen again. Also send Gage Carlisle a memo and ask that he be there. I trust his judgment as much as anyone else's."

She nodded. "Besides that, he knows when the best meals are served at the Red Lodge Café." She grinned up at him, remembering the stuffed flounder she and Gage had had for lunch and the teasing Gage had endured from Nan, the waitress there.

"Make reservations for us to be there two days. Let's be back here Friday night."

"Heavy date?" she asked and smiled as he grimaced.

"Business, unfortunately. We're going to have to start on that open house in Tahoe, too."

She told him about their trip then. "I had planned to get a preview of what it would be like, but the snow sent me home early."

"That was some storm. How'd you happen to get caught in it?" Her boss watched her carefully. She knew he hoped she and Ken would get back together if for no other reason than that he knew how much she'd loved Ken. What he didn't know was that Ken was determined to divorce her if she couldn't settle down and act the way *he* wanted her to act. Love me the way I want you to love me—or else—was Ken's way of thinking. She lifted her head and looked at Tom as he cleared his throat. He was waiting for her to tell him whom she was with, but she didn't mention Mike.

"Just a little ways below Minden there was a wreck, and we had to turn around and come back." She smiled for the first time. "With the help of snowplows, I might add." She didn't go into details about Bert being hurt and the ensuing rescue. Tom was sometimes like Ken when it came to believing she couldn't take care of herself, although he trusted her completely on the job. Relief caused her to sigh when he went on through the offices to his own private suite.

Wednesday would be May 8, and she sat there a few moments counting how far along in the early summer would be a good time for her to ask for vacation time. One of her trips into Red Lodge she planned to extend and go through some of the fabulous territory in Wyoming and Montana. May was a bit early; she would be taking a chance on another snowstorm that far north. In mid-June construction should be going full swing, and she could check on it and go adventuring, too. Alone, if she had to.

While married to Ken, Joy had always taken vacations during the summer while Penny was out of school, and that had been good enough for her, even though every place they went was crowded with families who had only summers free for vacations because of school-aged children.

She wasn't limited to summer vacations anymore; she was back to one-for-one and no one to look out for but herself. And she was already lonesome. Clenching her fists for a moment, she picked up the pen and began her foreword for the pamphlet she was preparing for the insurance company and brokers.

On the way home from work she stopped by the supermarket looking for something easy in the way of a quick meal.

"You don't need that one," a voice said near her shoulder, and she turned to face Ski and Paula. Ski, his injured arm fastened snugly against his chest, pointed to the frozen dinner she held, a Weight Watchers special.

"But it's easy and fast," she responded, smiling at the couple, unashamedly holding hands as they shopped.

"Come eat with us, Joy," Paula invited.

She looked down at the unappetizing package in her hand and accepted immediately. "If I can pay half the expenses," she said.

Paula shook her head. "It comes from a special fund that Ski and Mike contribute to a little at a time, and when they have a chance, which isn't often, I cook for them. Nothing fancy, just different from their fast-food menus."

Mike would be there. She hesitated but didn't know

how to say it might not be such a good idea for her to see very much of the intensely quiet policeman. The one whose kisses swept away her loneliness and doubt for a few earthshaking moments. He was very attractive, and she recognized how vulnerable she was at the moment. She was playing in the league of heartache with unwritten rules she didn't even remember.

Replacing the package in the freezer, she smiled at Paula. "Okay. I'll wash the dishes."

Following Paula's car down East Lane, she shook her head at the thought of spending a couple of hours with Mike again so soon. It was becoming a habit, and somehow she knew it was something that she shouldn't allow to happen. Somehow, she knew.

Paula turned into a driveway in front of a small bungalow set back from the street, and Joy slid out of her car to join them as they went around to the back door. Only Ski's car was in sight, and she was glad to have a few minutes to get settled before she would face Mike. Maybe the snowstorm was a lifesaver, getting her back to safe ground before she let herself get too close to another man. No more dependence on one for her; no more hurting because of any mere man.

Ski held the door open, and she walked through into the small kitchen and faced Mike across the room. Aside from a flicker of the gray eyes, his expression was as if he expected her.

"Hello, Joy," he said and smiled as he looked her over. "That color is much more becoming than olive drab." She held her breath as her glance locked with his, and both of them recalled the moments he saw her partially uncovered by the blanket.

"I'll say," Ski agreed enthusiastically, and she was suddenly glad she'd dressed in the light blue outfit, her hair caught in a heavy coil low on her neck, with soft tendrils in front of her ears.

"None the worse for wear?" Mike asked now.

"No. I took plenty of Vitamin C. Have you heard from Bert?" Perhaps Mike would never remark about the kiss and her warm response; she'd follow his lead.

"We went by the hospital this morning. He has a broken leg and a few cuts and bruises, and sends his heartfelt thanks."

She shuddered. "I'd forgotten snow could be so cold."

His look turned soft for a moment before he said, "Let's get out of the cook's way unless there's something we can help with?" He looked at Paula, who shook her head. "We'll wash dishes."

"I'm glad you said 'we,'" Joy told him, preceding him into the living room. "Where's Maude?"

He dropped into a big chair away from the couch where Joy sat. "She runs the shop on Mondays if Ski and I happen to have a couple of hours to eat."

"A couple of hours? You mean Ski is back on duty already?"

He grinned. "Nothing wrong with him except he can't drive. We have several guys laid up with the flu, and he came back to keep me company."

The conversation lagged, and she was beginning to get uncomfortable as Mike's gaze went over her several times, his eyes somehow calculating and distant, and she wondered what he was thinking. Perhaps he thought she'd planned to come here just to be near him. She opened her mouth to defend herself when Ski stuck his head in the door.

"Let's eat."

Joy listened to the conversation around her without saying much as they ate. It was an unfamiliar world they talked about, and she wasn't sure she wanted to know any more than she already did. Mike's expression closed as they discussed cases they were on, and she could see anger in his dark gray eyes. As they finished, she began gathering the dishes and stacking them on the counter.

"I was only kidding, Joy," Paula said. "We'll do these."

Ski looked hurt. "I thought I'd get out of this tonight."

"He really likes to wash dishes," Mike said, leaning against the counter. "It gets his fingernails clean."

They continued to kid one another as Joy started on the dishes. She looked up as Mike said, "Here. You need this." From somewhere he had gotten an apron and slipped the loop over her head and tied it behind her. For an instant, his hands tightened on her waist, and she looked around at him.

"Did you sleep well last night?" he asked unexpectedly.

She nodded. "As soon as I got warm, I went to sleep and didn't move till the alarm went off. How about you?" She wasn't going to tell him how warm she was when he left her and had no trouble keeping that warmth with her as she slipped into bed.

He dropped his hands and moved away from her. "Yes." His answer was short.

She concentrated on the warm, sudsy water as she washed the dishes. "I guess there's no way to find the guy that caused the wreck."

"You're right. He got away scot-free, as usual." His voice was carefully casual, no bitterness that she could detect, but she looked at him anyway. He was standing by the back door, staring out into the darkness. He straightened and came back to pick up the terry dish towel on the counter and started drying the dishes. They finished the job in silence and went back to join Ski and Paula in the living room. The couple stood close together, Ski's hands framing her face as Paula smiled at him. She was almost as tall as he, and she put her forehead against his chin.

Joy stopped and Mike bumped into her. His hand on her arm urged her into the room. "They don't know any better," he said.

Try as she would she couldn't decide what Mike's real feelings were—except he was a lot cooler toward her than he'd been Saturday and Sunday. Aside from the kiss she'd responded to so enthusiastically, she couldn't imagine what she'd done to cause the change in his attitude.

A few minutes later, she said, "Thanks for the dinner, Paula. It was much better than the one I'd picked for myself."

Paula walked with her to the door, and Joy called good night to the two men as she and Paula walked outside. "Drop by the coffee shop one night this week, Joy." She agreed and went on home alone.

THE MOMENT JOY WALKED through the doorway, Mike felt the familiar coiling of springs all through his body. He was beginning to suspect that somewhere in Joy's firmly packed body, she must have a built-in magnet made especially to cause a reaction inside his own. Under the very becoming blue outfit she wore, he pictured the bare shoulders and upthrust breasts that, for a moment, had come into his possession.

The shudder of remembrance was replaced by anger. There was no room in Mike Gresham's life for a woman like Joy Strayer, epitome of the feminine gentleness that required being taken care of. That made men want to protect her from the facts of life and all the evil that went with it. The kind of woman that a policeman who walked the streets of any city every day and night did *not* need.

All evening, he was careful not to touch her; all evening, he watched her covertly as she laughed and teased with them. There was still a look of uncertainty in her eyes, still a soft, vulnerable, "easy to hurt" appearance. He couldn't afford to get close to any woman who would be easy to hurt, and Joy Strayer fell into that category.

Not long after Joy left, he and Ski returned to duty, and he was caught up in the harrowing job of protecting the residents of Reno. For once he was glad to see the calls come one after the other; they kept his thoughts on less troublesome things.

Although, he admitted wryly to himself as he wrote up the last response, *I wouldn't exactly refer to Joy as a "thing."*

Chapter Twelve

The weather that had been bright and nippy following the storm turned warm and drizzly, and Joy stayed in the office as much as possible, eating a sandwich at her desk at lunchtime. Tom flew to South Carolina to see an old friend he'd graduated with from The Citadel. The friend was now an instructor at the famous military academy, and it had been five years since Tom's last trip there. She was rooting for them to have a fabulous time together as she remembered his enthusiasm about seeing his old college buddy. His demanding job was about all Tom really enjoyed, and she knew it would be good for him to be away from the taxing duties he insisted on performing. She wished he had invited her to go with him, immediately wondering what in the world she would do alone in a city like Charleston while he reminisced. She could be alone anywhere.

She shrugged away her bent toward self-pity and concentrated on her books. At six o'clock she sighed, closed her last ledger, and started home. Everyone

else had gone home at five and she walked through
the empty corridors, listening to her footsteps echo on
the shiny tile.

Outside the drizzle had stopped without much
moisture having fallen in the very dry climate where
they averaged less than four inches of rain per year.
She liked it that way, especially when she read about
all the snow and rain in other parts of the country.
January was usually Reno's nastiest month, and the
past weekend weather was a freak. She hoped it would
remain that way—a freak that happens only once in a
blue moon.

Tourist season was already picking up. Traffic was
heavy north of her on Virginia Boulevard, where casinos stayed open twenty-four hours a day, and, even
in midweek, entertainment was lavish and star-
studded. Things of that nature held little interest for
her, but it brought plenty of revenue for the city and
state.

Just south of the main casino district, she could see
the gold angles of the dome of the Pioneer Theater Au-
ditorium, where conventions were held. The building
fascinated her because Tom had designed it, and she
had spent many days wandering through the underground portion that extended beneath the entrance ter-
race. From the outside it appeared small; inside, it was
tremendous.

She turned into her driveway and parked in her
usual spot, her footsteps slow as she went into the
building, stopping long enough to remove her mail.
The telephone was ringing as she unlocked the door

and went in, leaning for a moment against it before she moved to pick up the receiver.

"Joy?" She went still at the sound of Ken's voice. "I've been calling for over an hour. Are you working late again?"

It was an automatic response as she said, "Only an hour," defending herself as always against his criticism of her habits.

There was a silence on the line as she waited to see why he had called her. "Did you get the letter about the divorce?" he asked finally.

"Yes." There was nothing she could add to that.

He cleared his throat. "Is that all you have to say?"

A streak of stubbornness helped with her short answers. "Yes."

He spoke again after a rather long silence between them. "If you're going to contest the divorce, you'll have to appear in court sometime this month."

"I know."

"Are you?" he insisted.

"No." She stared at the doorknob.

After another awkward silence, he asked, "Is there anything you want from the house?"

From Sharon's house? "No, Ken. Everything there is yours. If you find anything of mine, please discard it." She stiffened in anger and asked, "How long until the divorce is final?"

"Six weeks." Ken's voice sounded far away. He had withdrawn his sympathetic questioning and was willing to let her go her headstrong way. And that was where she was going—alone.

A moment later, he said a stilted good-bye, and she replaced the receiver to stand looking down at it. Her indrawn breath was shaky as she went into the bedroom and pulled the old faithful T-shirt from the drawer and hung her clothes in the closet and turned to find something to eat.

TOM RETURNED TO THE OFFICE on Friday afternoon, tanned and rested. She stared. "You look wonderful. Did you find a new romance?" Only Joy could get away with that line of questioning.

He grinned. "I feel good because I look ten years younger than Bergstrom. That job is killing him. I told him he needed to come to the wide-open spaces and breathe some clean air." He looked her over and nodded. "Everything all right here?"

"Yes." She didn't answer the real question he was asking, but he gave her a long look and went on into his office.

A few minutes later, she followed him with the memo she wrote daily to let him know what was going on in her bailiwick. He was a boss who wanted to keep his eye on progress or changes in his company, and she believed in keeping him informed. Through the years, he had come to depend on that from her, and she didn't disappoint him.

"I talked to Mayor Sangen, and he'll be looking for us next Wednesday. The flight gets into Billings in the afternoon now instead of late evening, and he said he'd meet us there for dinner."

"Fine." He was already engrossed in her memo,

and she went back to her desk to finish a column of figures he'd need to review before they left Reno.

When he emerged from his office, after everyone else had gone, he said, "Joy, don't you have anything to occupy your time besides this job?" As soon as he asked the question, he realized it didn't sound just right, but he stood glaring at her just the same.

She smiled at him, knowing he would never intentionally say anything to hurt her. "No, as a matter of fact, I don't."

He looked down at her as he buttoned his suit coat and said, "I have something for you in the car. Let's go."

She gathered up the papers she had, picked up another file along with her handbag, and walked out of the building with him. He gave her a resigned look as he saw the work she was taking home.

"Let's drop your car off at your apartment and eat before you go slave for that boss of yours."

When she opened her mouth to protest, he said, "If I don't feed you, you won't eat, and the next few weeks on this Red Lodge project are going to require lots of energy and, as much as I hate to admit it, overtime along with it."

She pulled out from the parking lot with his car following close behind her and a few minutes later parked at her apartment building. He opened the door for her to get into his car and pulled away without speaking. She looked over the seat at a plain box.

He grunted. "Wait until you get it in the house to open it."

"Peekaboo lingerie from Frederick's?" she teased. He never failed to bring her a memento from wherever he went, usually earrings or something small she could use. Nothing he brought her had ever come in such a big box, and she was naturally curious.

He gave her a quick grin and concentrated on his driving through Friday evening traffic. Tourists were already heading for the gambling casinos and big-name shows their city sported. The quiet steak house where he stopped was one of their favorite after-work eateries.

They ordered and she looked around at the diners, bringing her glance back to him as he asked suddenly, "Are you separated from Ken permanently?"

Swallowing over the lump in her throat, she said, "He's filing for divorce." Her soft mouth twisted. "He doesn't believe in dragging things out."

After a long silence while he watched her expression, he said, "Are you giving him up without a fight?"

"If you mean will I contest the divorce, no, I won't. Ken doesn't need me, or he would never have let me leave the house in the first place."

"What about Penny?" He knew well the affection she had for the pretty little girl so long without a mother.

"They have each other." She looked up at him. "One day Ken will find someone who won't notice he lives with two women, and he'll marry again." She'd shared Ken with a memory; someone else would do the same. She shivered with remembered pain and sat back in her chair. "Don't worry about me, Tom. I can manage alone."

The gray-haired man staring at the dark-haired girl opposite him didn't look much different from any of the other diners; and Joy knew that if they bothered to think about it at all, most of them would assume that the old man had himself a young girlfriend. She smiled at the thought and looked up as their meal was served.

As they began to eat, she switched the subject to Red Lodge, and they spent an hour discussing their upcoming visit and what they could expect. That was one good thing about Tom and her—they could talk for hours without getting bored with each other. The animated conversation took them through the meal, and they were still on their favorite subject of Red Lodge as they walked out to his car.

As he stopped in front of her apartment, Tom reached into the backseat to get the box for her and walked to her door, waiting as she unlocked it.

He grinned at her as he handed the box to her. "It's big enough for you to get lost in, just the way you like them." As he pulled the door to behind him, he said, "Good night, Joy."

Placing the box on the bed, she jounced it a few times until the top came off. Inside was the brightest orange knit shirt she had ever seen. She pulled it out to inspect it and laughed out loud.

On the back of the T-shirt were big black printed letters of the South Carolina Clemson Tigers, and covering the front was a huge black tiger paw. Strip-

ping off her clothes, she promptly slipped the shirt
over her head and looked at herself in the mirror.
Loose-fitting enough to hide the curves beneath, it
fell almost to her knees. The black pad of the paw lay
across her middle, and the four claws made a half-
circle over the barely discernible shape of her breasts.

Twisting to see the back, she smiled at CLEMSON low
on her shoulders and TIGERS across her hips, their
shape almost completely hidden by the folds of the
big shirt. Perfect fit. Not many bosses would buy
oversized T-shirts for their marketing consultants, but
then few female employees had bosses like Tom Conan.

IT WAS NINE O'CLOCK the next morning when the door
bell rang. Joy, still dressed in the Clemson Tigers
shirt, was up with the Red Lodge ledgers spread over
the small table, a cup of coffee in her hand. She
frowned as she looked toward the door, not wanting
in the least to be disturbed. "Who is it?" she demanded in a none-too-friendly voice.

"It's Mike, Joy. I came to pick up the blanket."

Staring at the door and startled at the voice answering her, she slid the lock back and opened the door to
look up at Mike, completely forgetting her state of
dress. Or undress.

Not until she saw the grin across his face as his eyes
went over her figure did she realize how she must
look.

"Oh," she said and stepped back. "Come in,
Mike." She pushed the door closed and leaned against

it. "I'm sorry, but I was working and not expecting anyone."

His gray gaze continued to go over the figure in front of him, and she felt the red color stain her face. Her hair hadn't been brushed, and she was barefoot.

Her chin lifted as she stepped around Mike to move toward the hassock, where she had placed the blanket she wore home from their misadventure in the snowstorm—and which had eventually partially unveiled her body for Mike to see—and touch. She turned to face him, her good manners asserting themselves in spite of her informal dress and even more informal thoughts.

"Would you like a cup of coffee, Mike?"

He was still standing near the door holding his policeman's hat in one hand. His dark hair, brushed back from his face, showed the strands of gray spread generously through the thick waves. Clean-shaven, standing tall in the neat blue uniform, Mike gave the appearance of strength. She knew that strength from the feel of his hands on her, lifting her when she was too drunk to stand, lifting her from the sidewalk to take her to the hospital, lifting Bert as a deadweight from the seat of the truck. Her gaze went from big hands, holding the hat in front of him, back to meet his look.

He shook his head. "Ski's waiting for me. We wanted to drop the blanket off at the hospital as we go by to see Bert. I understand he's going home today."

"I'm glad." She smiled as she picked up the blanket to hand it to him. "He shouldn't have any more snowstorms to fight until next winter, at least."

Mike placed his hat on his head, cocked at a jaunty angle, and took the blanket from her. He looked down at her, unsmiling for a moment. A sudden grin showed even white teeth.

"That color is very becoming, Joy. You should wear it more often." He waved good-bye, and she heard his footsteps moving quickly down the hall as she pushed the door closed and locked it.

He was in a hurry to leave, but of course Ski was waiting for him. Disturbed by the brief visit, she found it hard to return to her papers and sat at the table with a fresh cup of coffee, staring at nothing. Her finger traced a pattern on the Formica top of the small dinette table as she thought about her two years with Ken and Penny. They were over, to be written off as experience.

Out of nowhere came lines she'd read somewhere, in some long-forgotten magazine or newspaper article, and memorized because they appealed to her, even before she knew Ken. Perhaps she'd known, even then, that one day she'd need the words to guide her, to back her up when she was going down for the third time.

How did the lines go? She frowned, trying to remember the words that had impressed her so at the time. But after all this time, she couldn't recall the exact words. The gist of the quote was accepting defeats with head up, eyes open, with the grace of a woman, not the sorrow of a child. *Which am I,* she wondered, *woman or child? Each is equally vulnerable when it comes to loving and being hurt.* And what else was in the article? Construct the roads on the here and now because anything else is too uncertain. Yeah, tomorrow never comes, they say. *Funny,* she thought now, *my tomorrows have a way of coming too quickly.*

Okay, so I build my life on solid ground; no quicksand, no unexpected washing away of the things I thought solidly mine. And, if nothing else, I'll learn from past mistakes, learn that Joy can be depended on in the absence of someone else. The exact quote still eluded her, but it had mentioned that whether you realized it or not, you're strong and you have worth; with every disappointment and trial by fire, you learn and learn and...

"You're strong and you have worth," she repeated the line aloud, smiling grimly as she did so. "I'm not strong, and I need someone to tell me I'm worth a little something."

She stood up and took her cup to the sink to rinse it. Enough philosophizing, enough regret, enough past—on to the future.

"I don't need anyone," she reassured herself and, lifting her chin, went back to her papers. There was a mountain of work to be finished before next Wednesday and the trip with Tom into Montana.

Chapter Thirteen

Their successful trip to Red Lodge behind them, Joy settled down to work out the detailed computer programs that would give Tom and the representatives of the small town a clear picture of what had happened and what was to come as construction progressed on the dam. Related projects spawned by insight into the changes that would be needed later must be incorporated into her programs and figures.

Overtime became a way of life, and she had little time to brood over the upcoming divorce. Sometimes, late at night, she would wake to twist and turn in her misery, but with the light of day she repeated grimly to herself: *Accept your defeats, head up, eyes open. You have strength—remember?* Sometimes it was hard, but stubbornly she lifted her head and opened her eyes wide, hoping nothing else would sneak up on her to throw her for a loop.

It was a gorgeous bright blue June day. Grocery shopping had priority because she'd been grabbing something to and from work, not cooking at all except an occasional breakfast. Frequenting the coffee shop where Paula worked became a regular habit.

Joy had slept late that day, unusual for her, and Saturday morning shoppers were already ahead of her in the supermarket. But she was in no hurry and loitered in the aisles of the store, reading labels she never took time to look at, much less read. At the ice-cream section, she looked for a small box of strawberry and found strawberry topping to go with it. Close by were the whipped creams and walnut toppings she loved.

I'll have to play tennis all day tomorrow to work this off, she thought gleefully as she put the additional items in her basket.

"You're really indulging yourself, aren't you?" a teasing voice asked, and she looked up to see Ski and Paula.

"Yep. I deserve it," she said. "And how did you manage a Saturday off?" she asked, looking at Ski.

It was Paula who laughed as she answered her. "Don't panic. He'll be back on the street looking out for us by noon."

Joy shook her head. "You people have the craziest hours."

"To match our crazy job," Ski told her.

She wanted to ask where his partner was, but the better part of valor kept her from doing so. They talked a few minutes and then went their separate ways.

From noon till when, she wondered as she checked out. Since it was Saturday, they might be relieved anywhere from eight that night till noon the next day, according to how vicious the people they protected became through the passing hours.

She thought of all the wives and girlfriends waiting anxious hours for a call or an appearance of their men. Were they all as strong as Mike said policemen's families and friends should be? Endurance was a fact of life for them and strength a necessity.

At three o'clock, she went to the tennis courts and found a partner in the person of a bored tourist with whom she played two sets and was back in her apartment by five, ready to resume work that she wanted to finish before returning to work Monday morning. There was never time at the office to study the program in detail and to concentrate as she needed to do on the complicated figures.

Taking her mail with her as she entered the apartment, she laid it on the table by the couch and went on into the bedroom. Stripping off her tennis shorts and shirt, she showered and slipped the orange Clemson Tigers shirt over her head on her way to the kitchen to fix a sandwich.

Appetite whetted by the strenuous game of tennis, she completed her lunch with a bowl of ice cream, topped by whipped cream and walnuts, sighing as she finished. She yawned and stretched.

Maybe I'll take a nap before I go back to work, she thought, checking to see that it was almost seven o'clock, really too late for a nap. She picked up the letters from the table, pulling her bare feet up under her as she sat on the couch to go through them.

The envelope was there among some other, uninteresting literature, the return address that of the familiar law firm. A chill passed through her, but she opened the flap and removed the letter, reading all of it before she put it down beside her. The divorce, uncontested, was final, and she was a free woman again. Ken and Penny wiped from her life as if they never existed.

She got off the couch and stretched on the floor, doing sit-ups and leg lifts to relax the muscles knotted throughout her body. When the phone rang, she turned her head to look up at it without moving or making any effort to answer it, mentally counting the times it rang before it finally ceased its strident sound. The silence was forbidding, and she wished it would ring again, but it didn't.

Her forlorn hope that nothing else would sneak up on her had been useless, but she should have been watching for this blow, knowing that it was coming. Perhaps she thought if she ignored the problem, it would go away.

Snatches of the half-forgotten quote reached out to her. "With each good-bye, you learn." What? What does divorce teach you? It was a sort of defeat, and you accept defeat with the strength of a real woman, not the sorrow of a child.

But her sorrow would not be denied, and she felt the wetness of her tears as they filled her eyes and ran down her cheeks into her mouth, salty and bitter. She let them fall until her nose stopped up and she was forced to find a tissue to mop some of the excess moisture from her face. Taking another tissue, she blew her nose until she could breathe again; then she got up to put the saturated pieces of thin paper in the garbage.

As she turned toward the bedroom, the door bell rang. Muttering at the interruption of her misery, she stalked to the door.

"Who is it?" she demanded, her voice harsh from the choking sensation left by tears continuing to fall even as she stood there. She let them run down her cheeks, unheeded, and stood waiting for an answer from the opposite side of the door.

"Mike."

Somehow that one word set her off. She flung the door open. "And what do you want, Mike?"

He was leaning against the door frame and straightened in surprise when the door opened with such force. Gray eyes took in the figure in front of him, defiant and tearstained. He had never seen her angry, and the blazing eyes shot blue fire at him as she waited for an excuse for his unscheduled appearance.

In civilian clothes Mike was just as good-looking as ever, and for some reason that infuriated her. "Well?" she asked, not moving from the doorway.

"What's wrong, Joy?" he asked.

"Wrong? What makes you think there's anything wrong, Mike?" She flung her arm at nothing in particular, still without moving from his path.

He took hold of her arms and pushed her back into the room, following her and shoving the door closed behind him. "Yes, I asked what's wrong. Now, tell me."

Whirling away from him, she stumbled, unable to see because of the tears, and took a swipe across her eyes with the sleeve of the Clemson shirt. Thick and absorbent, it did a good job of smearing the tears over her face. She sniffed and reached for more tissues to blow her nose.

Facing away from him, she said, "Go away, Mike. Just go away."

"Not until you tell me why you're crying."

"Have you read the headlines in the paper today?" she asked, her voice muffled.

"No, why? What's in them to make you cry like this?"

"I don't know, but there must be something on the front page worth crying over."

"You aren't making any sense, Joy," he told her. He caught her arms and turned her to face him. She stared up at him, her lips working to hold back the sobs building in her throat, swallowing the tears that kept running into her mouth.

Feathery black lashes were stuck together in pointed stars, the blue of the irises seeming to fill her entire eyes, the jet-black pupils swimming in her tears. Her nose wiggled as she tried to control the muscles working in her cheeks, fighting to hold back the sobs.

"Nothing can be that bad." He smiled down at her as he spoke, and she jerked away from him.

After a few seconds, her voice calmer, she said, "You're right, Mike." She turned away and went to sit down on the couch, drawing her left foot up under her. The long orange shirt covered the bare essentials, but she didn't even think about it. At the moment, she didn't care.

He remained standing, looking down at the disconsolate figure, freshly shampooed dark hair falling forward to hide part of one cheek, the other side tucked behind her ear. The streaks of her tears shone in the dim light from the one lamp.

"Did you get the divorce papers?" he asked.

She nodded without asking how he knew. He had only to look at her and know that was all she needed to present such a sorry appearance.

"And you're still crying over him? Why?" Mike's voice was hard as he stood over her. "You knew it was coming, Joy. It isn't as if it's a great big surprise, so why are you crying at this late date?"

Big, strong Mike.

She looked up at him, seeing accusing gray eyes as he sought to arrest her for drunken driving, saw steely gray eyes darkened with anger as he saw all that should be done in a policeman's twenty-four-hour day that judges frequently ruined by setting the guilty free on technicalities. Mike was condemning her in the same way he would look upon anyone who in a careless moment did something against the law. She was breaking the law, letting something so common as a divorce get the best of her. Mike was innocent of ever breaking a heart or of having his broken, simply because he couldn't be bothered with getting involved with a woman weak enough to love.

"I'm going to cry until I can't cry anymore, Mike. I plan to cry all I have to tonight, and tomorrow I'll accept whatever comes; accept it as a woman should. But tonight—tonight is my time to cry." A blink of the long lashes let loose more tears, but she went on. "And I'll find out just how strong I am." She stood up. "Go home, Mike. I'm not strong like you are; I want my chance to be weak without being condemned for it. After all—" she smiled through the tears "—I never really claimed to be strong enough for you, and if I ever get my head up enough to stop the tears, I'll be okay. It takes more time for me than for some people, but people die from gunshot wounds, from traffic accidents, even from pneumonia, but not of broken hearts." She was no longer sure if she had a broken heart; perhaps it was just badly bent, and scarred pride had something to do with her feelings.

"I never thought I'd see you wallow in self-pity," he said tightly.

"Take a good look; you won't see it again," she said as she walked toward the bedroom. "Please lock the door on your way out."

He watched her walk away from him, reading the print on the back of the orange knit shirt. He was enough of a football fan to recognize the Clemson Tigers. Heavy waves of black hair swung on her shoulders and the black lettering wavered with the movement of her hips beneath the shirt.

He reached her with one step and turned her to face him. "Joy, I'm sorry," he said, pulling her close.

Even as she stood there, her wet face drenched his shirt front as she leaned against him. He led her back to the couch and pulled her down with him, cuddling her to his chest. He took a handful of tissues and wiped at the tears and held it to her nose.

"Blow," he ordered. She did, and he threw the tissues on the table and took another handful. She gulped, trying to hold back the tears and succeeded only in a strangled sob that set off another wave of crying. He held her as her body shook, and a long time later she lay still, with only an occasional jerk as the sobs subsided and finally ceased altogether.

Looking down into the mottled face, red all around her eyes, he found she had gone to sleep, emotionally exhausted. Smiling, he lifted her to carry her, childlike, into her bedroom.

Turning back the old red spread, he placed her on the sheets, but when he was moving away, Joy whispered, "Don't leave me."

Mike lay down with her, pillowing her head on his arm. She moved close, her face burrowed in his shirt front, her fingers slipped between two of the buttons. Her sigh sent a shudder through her slender frame, and his arms tightened around her.

JOY WOKE SLOWLY, conscious of a heaviness across her stomach. She tried to move, but something was holding her down. Bringing her hands up, she pushed at the weight only to have it tighten, turning her to a warm body.

Her breath caught as she stared into Mike's face on her pillow. He was asleep, thick lashes settled on his cheek, firm lips closed, breathing easily through his nose. A dark shadow of beard made his complexion seem darker than she remembered, but she had never been this close to him with time to observe the planes of his face, the even texture of his skin.

Lord, she thought, *how did this happen?* The events of the evening marched past in her mind—the divorce decree; Mike's arrival; her crying jag that went on and on until he put her to bed and stayed with her at her own request. He was still fully dressed, but the Tigers shirt had crept up around her hips, and she couldn't get her hands free to push it down.

Panicky, she tried to ease out of his arms, and suddenly she was looking into dark gray eyes lit with surprise.

Their gaze locked for several seconds, neither of them speaking; then he smiled and asked softly, "Okay?"

"Yes." Her voice was barely audible.

In the half-light of early morning, his eyes changed as he whispered, "Joy," pulling her fully into his arms.

She lay relaxed in the protective circle for an instant but quickly turned on her back to slide away from him. His arms didn't yield, and she was pulled back on the pillow. One hand came up to catch her chin and hold it as he raised himself on an elbow, bending to place warm lips on hers. His kiss had a temporarily tranquilizing effect on her, and she stopped trying to move away from him. She belonged in his embrace for that one moment until she could get the strength to face what was to come.

As she lay there, his mouth moved along her jaw

line to the pulse hammering in her throat, on to the
hollow in her shoulder, where he pushed the shirt
aside. A quiver trembled through her body as he
trailed a line of kisses from the hollow downward.

"No." She tugged at his shoulders. "Mike, please."

He raised his head to look down into the dark pools
of blue, lowering his head again to find her soft
mouth, smothering her protests. One hand fit her
waist, curving over the rounded hip, crossing the flat-
ness of her stomach, lying there, still, except for the
long fingers that caressed over her hipbone.

For a moment more, she struggled, then her lips
parted as she responded with the desire he roused in
her, moaning as he whispered to her. Her body arched
beneath the gentle massage of his hands, moving
under him as he pulled the shirt over her head. He
held her to his hard body, softly stroking the smooth
skin of her hips and belly. With every move of his
hands, he kissed her—the curve of her cheek where
the dimples showed, her eyelids closed against the
passion he roused in her. He murmured her name as
she answered his hard kiss, letting his hands move to
separate her firm thighs, bringing their bodies together. She drowned in the sweetness of his love,
holding him close as his fiery kiss gave him complete
possession over her.

Chapter Fourteen

The gurgling of the coffee maker was the only sound in the small kitchen as she stood gazing into the shining stainless-steel sink. Her body seemed something apart from her physically, bound by the strength of Mike holding her.

She turned at the sound of Mike's footsteps as he came from the bedroom, and they stared at each other. His lips were pressed together in a straight line, and she stiffened at the wariness in his face. The look in his eyes could have been anything, but mostly she saw the guarded expression that meant he wasn't sure what to say. She smiled.

"Coffee will be ready in a couple of minutes. You'll have time for a cup before you have to go. Would you like some scrambled eggs?" Her voice sounded the same as she remembered it from the day before, much to her surprise.

"Just a cup of coffee." He stood by the table, watching her. "I'm sorry, Joy." The words came slowly, his voice faltering over the apology.

Reaching for the two cups she had placed on the counter, she didn't look at him as she said, "So am I, Mike." She bit her lip but went on before she lost her ability to speak at all. "Since we both know it shouldn't have happened, we can act like adults and not get hysterical."

She felt hysterical. Her divorce barely final, she'd heaped another mistake on top of that. Grim laughter threatened to bubble up from her aching throat as she recalled the lines she had so diligently decided to use as her theme song: "And you learn and learn...." She'd learned nothing and most likely never would. "Head up and eyes open." Oh, yes, her eyes were open without seeing anything, and strength...somewhere she'd find it. And Mike...well, Mike could take care of himself.

"It isn't the end of the world, you know," he said.

She nodded and smiled. "It's all right, Mike. I know what you're trying to say, and I'm telling you it's all right."

She poured coffee and gave him the cup, trying not to flinch as their fingers touched, aware of the desire to walk into his arms to be held close again. They shared an awkward silence as neither attempted more conversation.

He finished the coffee and put the cup in the sink as he turned back to her. "Take care, Joy," he said, and kissed her cheek on his way to the door.

Locking the door behind him as he left, she leaned against it, head back, eyes closed. Again she felt Mike's arms around her, his mouth on hers loving her for a short while, but at least he'd loved her when she was in need of love, temporary though his love might be.

She didn't know what had prompted him to stop by her apartment on a Saturday night, remembering only that she had attacked him before he could say anything. What happened after that was a total disaster.

Her moves around the apartment were automatic. Without seeing any of the items she picked up and placed out of sight, she went through the room, avoiding the bedroom where the tumbled bed reminded her too much of Mike.

As she straightened the cushions on the couch, she heard the rustle of paper and pushed them apart to see the first letter from the divorce lawyer. She picked it up and stood looking at the wrinkled pages, turning to put them in the garbage can in the kitchen. The cover fell to with a solid clank, a sound of finality to a finished subject.

MIKE WATCHED THE SLOW MOVEMENT of the door as it swung shut behind him. It isn't the end of the world, he'd told Joy. Then why did he feel so empty? Why did everything seem so unfinished? His glib reassurance to her didn't ring true even to him; how must she feel right now?

Strongly tempted to knock on the door, go back and sweep her into his arms, he stood there. To hell with being early on a shift that would probably last twelve hours anyway. Let someone else assume responsibility for a while. He still wanted Joy with an urgency he couldn't recall in years. He lifted his hand toward the door, then let it drop. *Leave well enough alone, Mike; you've done enough damage for one day.*

Ski didn't notice much difference about his quiet partner as they drove through the downtown area, past the casinos full of the same people they'd left there the day before—or some just like them. He turned the car on a back street and headed for the coffee shop.

She's so fragile, Mike was thinking, for once his mind not on the job he took so seriously. His mind was full of Joy Strayer. Uncertainty wasn't a characteristic he was familiar with. He made his life-and-death decisions in the flash of an eye and, right or wrong, he was stuck with them. But now, with his arms still feeling the softness of Joy in them, he was filled with uncertainty.

Making love to her was an unplanned thing, and he wanted to shrug his shoulders and forget about it. Forget the misery in her blue eyes as she turned to him to hold her. Forget the smell of her hair, the whisper of her breath on his cheek, her automatic resistance as he held her tightly. Forget the sweetness of her response as she surrendered to him, giving what he demanded with an intensity to match his own.

Joy Strayer wasn't the woman for Mike Gresham, of that he was positive. There were lovely women for him to date when his schedule permitted, one of whom would probably make a good wife for a dedicated policeman; but he couldn't bring himself to tie any woman to the everyday fact of life that he might not live till midnight. Phyllis Gresham had been one who stuck it out till the day his father didn't come home. She'd never exhibited any bitterness about being left to raise a small boy alone, and when he chose to be a policeman, she never objected. But few women had the stamina his mother had, he was certain.

He knew Joy dreaded the divorce—perhaps she was feeling guilt over a failed marriage. It happened every day, hundreds of times a day in Reno. Where was her family? God, he'd never inquired about her life. All he'd noticed about her was the blue-violet of her eyes, the dark hair so black that it, too, reflected midnight blue at times. And the weakness that went with small, pretty females who needed someone to look after them twenty-four hours a day.

"If you'd rather I not talk to you, just say so," Ski said, and Mike turned to look at him. "I've been talking for five minutes, to myself, I guess, since you seem to be preoccupied."

"Sorry, Ski, what did you say?" He pushed Joy Strayer to the back of his mind; he didn't need any more distractions on the streets today.

"Ready to go see Paula?"

Mike nodded. "I can use some good strong coffee."

THE DAY WAS A WASTE for Joy. She tried to work, but the printed figures in her ledgers ran together, and her fingers gripped the pen so hard they ached. She gave up, put on a jogging outfit, and struck out at a brisk trot across the street to the park a few blocks away. She ran until she dropped onto a bench, breath coming fast, legs trembling with the exertion.

Her thoughts tangled around Mike, and she shook her head, looking up at the clear blue of the sky, not a cloud in sight. All the clouds and dark thunderheads were inside her mind. From her long-ago Sunday school lessons she remembered a passage that said in part: "And this, too, shall pass."

I'm not sure I'll last long enough for it to pass, she thought, and got up to walk slowly home.

The apartment hadn't changed; it was empty. Empty of feelings except for her own restless questions. Empty of the love that Mike had taken with him.

Love. No, no, not that. Mike had no room in his life for a woman he considered too weak to survive there.

"It isn't the end of the world." Her own voice startled her as she repeated the words Mike had said. She'd take his word for it.

Ignoring the fact that she hadn't eaten all day, she drank a glass of milk and ate two cookies. Taking an extra blanket from the closet, she took her pillow from the bed, refusing to look at it except briefly, and fixed herself a place to sleep in the living room. The bedroom was haunted, not by her former husband anymore, but by a dark-haired policeman too brave for her to be in the same league.

"I can't believe I'm so stupid," she said aloud to the ceiling above her. "Tom would fire me on the spot if I used as poor judgment in business as I do in my personal life." She would be the last to tell him.

Of necessity she went into the bedroom the next morning to dress, averting her gaze from the bed where she had slept in Mike's arms. Everywhere she looked, she saw his eyes, condemning her for being weak. He couldn't imagine anyone being unable to accept whatever life handed him—your cards are dealt and you play your hand. Sergeant Gresham's rules of the game.

Leaving the apartment early, she drove down the main street where the coffee shop was located and parked nearby, breathing in the warm breeze of the quiet Monday morning. Most of the tables and booths inside the shop were full, and she slid onto an empty stool at the counter. Paula saw her from the back and waved.

"How're things, Joy?" she asked as she took her order.

Joy smiled, wondering briefly what Paula would say if she told her just how things really were with her. "Fine. I was too lazy to fix my own breakfast and hadn't seen you in a few days, either, so I used that as an excuse to come by."

Someone called Paula, and with a quick grin she left to see what was needed. Joy finished her breakfast and called out a "see you later" to Paula as she left.

For a moment, she sat still behind the wheel of her car, looking over the near-empty street, already freshly cleaned by city employees, drew a deep breath, and turned toward Conan's. She had to work for a living no matter what. She hoped the day would be so hectic that she wouldn't have time to think about Mike or Ken or Penny or, least of all, about Joy. Mike was right. It had been long enough in coming that the blow should have been cushioned by time. The hurt was there, but it would mend, leaving only scars that would soon disappear.

Her wish was granted, and at six-thirty that evening she stood up and stretched, rubbing the tense muscles at the back of her neck. She didn't want to go home and headed her car in the direction of the tennis courts.

Taking her racquet from the trunk of the car, she went to change into black shorts and white knit shirt and walked around the end of the benches looking for someone without a partner.

To her surprise, the same bored tourist she'd found on Friday was there, staring gloomily at the figures moving energetically around him. As she stopped in front of him, the man looked up. She didn't even know his name.

The scowl left his face and he grinned. "I didn't dare hope you'd be back here today."

"Bad day at the office, and I need to beat the tar out of something. What better than a little tennis?" She swung her racquet.

He stood beside her, a tall angular man past middle age, but slim and straight. "My name is Dan Corvair, from Washington, D.C." He extended his hand.

"Joy Strayer, Reno." She took the hand and smiled at him.

"You mean you're a native?"

"From day one," she told him.

He grinned. "I thought everyone was a tourist like me."

"Not quite everyone."

He shook his head as he looked around them. "This time of year in Washington is right nice, but in a few weeks it will be so hot and sticky, you can't breathe. Maybe I should have waited a little later to visit here."

"It gets hot here, Mr. Corvair, but not sticky. We barely get enough rain to dampen the spirits." For a moment she remembered a snowstorm not many weeks ago, but that was south of Reno, and a freak at that, not to be counted—except for the memories.

Taking out her frustration on the little yellow ball and Mr. Corvair, Joy beat him soundly the first set and gave in only a little on the second. They dropped onto the benches, breathing hard.

As they settled down, he turned to her. "How about some dinner, Joy?"

The empty apartment would wait for her. "If you aren't interested in a fancy place, I know where we can get a decent meal without going into hock for it," she told him.

He agreed, and she went to change clothes, coming back to get into her car. "Follow me. It isn't far from us."

Inside the coffee shop, she smiled at the surprise on Paula's face as she led them to a booth. "Paula, a visitor to our fair city, Dan Corvair, of Washington,

D.C., although he denies any responsibility for what goes on there." Paula gave him her quick grin and friendly nod as she moved away.

"Are you a gambling man, Mr. Corvair?"

He put up his hand. "Please. You beat me bad enough that you could at least call me by my first name."

Her dimples flashed. "All right, Dan."

He leaned back in the booth. "I've played the machines a little, but I really came out to reminisce." At her questioning look, he laughed a little. "My wife and I were married in Reno during World War Two, and we always meant to come back here. It was just a small town back then and the best place to get married in a hurry." He moved the fork near his plate and looked up to meet her interested gaze. "Kitty died two years ago, and I decided I'd come back here just for her."

"I'm glad Reno has good memories for you," she said.

He nodded. "Everywhere I lived with Kitty has good memories."

My goodness, she thought, *some people don't even mind admitting marriage is good for them.* Mike would be vastly surprised to learn that you didn't have to be afraid of losing someone if you had the good memories to sustain you.

As if conjured up by her thoughts, she glanced up to meet Mike's dark gaze as he stood near the counter. Ski was there, too, talking to Paula. He touched Mike's arm and sat down, but Mike continued to glare at her, his eyes going from her to Dan Corvair.

Her water glass, lifted to her lips, suddenly jiggled, and she put it down on the table while her mind sent an instant replay of the night in Mike's arms through her, leaving her weak. She smiled at him, her tongue touching her crooked tooth, but he turned his back and sat at the counter with Ski. His cool rejection of her was plain enough to shake her all the way to her toes.

She stared at his back, realizing anew what had happened. Without being aware of danger, she'd turned to Mike for comfort in her misery, and he'd moved without any trouble into a heart searching for happiness. She was going to pay double for being so unwary.

She looked at the table. *I get the message, Mike,* she thought, hurting the way he meant for her to hurt.

Paula placed their dinners in front of them, and she listened to Dan as he talked about his travels with Kitty, the smaller apartment he'd taken in Washington after her death.

"Come visit me and I'll show you around. There's lots of history even if you don't like big cities." She came back to what he was saying.

"My boss sends me everywhere but Washington, Dan," she told him. "He keeps that part for himself."

He laughed. "I'll have to meet that boss of yours and talk to him."

"Tom Conan of Conan Enterprises."

"Dams and things?"

"Yes, that's right," she said, surprised.

"I read an article about him in the business section of the *Washington Post* not long ago, about a project he's backing somewhere up north."

She leaned forward. "Yes. Red Lodge, Montana. Beautiful small town."

They went on talking, and she tried to ignore Mike's broad back at the counter. He was gone when they got up to leave.

Outside, Dan Corvair extended his hand. "I'll be leaving early tomorrow, Joy. It's been a pleasure. If you do come to Washington, look me up. I'm in the book."

Joy waited by her car as he got into his rented one, and she looked around to see if, by chance, Mike and Ski were still in the area. The patrol car wasn't in sight.

At home, she stood uncertainly in the middle of the living room, hunched her shoulders and walked into the bedroom. *I can't stay out of it forever hiding from a ghost that doesn't exist,* she decided resolutely.

The bed was still rumpled in its unmade state, the way she and Mike had left it. Near the foot of the bed was the orange Tigers shirt. She shut her eyes tightly for a moment, then clamping her teeth together, she went to work, stripping the linens from the bed, rolling them together with the T-shirt and throwing them all into the hamper.

In the bathroom she gathered the towels they had used, replacing them from the closet. Unaccustomed to male usage, the small room had a different smell and feel, and she looked around, trying to figure out what it was that made it different. The mirror was the same, wiped clean of any mist from the shower. The drawers were pushed closed, everything now neat and in its rightful place. Only Mike's presence remained.

She pushed the light switch and went back into the bedroom to pull fresh sheets from the chest, dusted the furniture with a few swipes of lemon oil and went back into the living room. The apartment was small, even for her, and now it was crowded with memories.

Once again she was alone and on her own. From this day forward, it would be that way. All that remained for her to do was keep Mike in the right perspective and go on with her life.

Chapter Fifteen

Corporal Paraski slowed the patrol car for the stop-
light and turned to look at his partner. Sergeant Mike
Gresham, a legend in his own time with the Reno
Police Department. Together they patrolled the mean-
est beat in Reno, where Mike's father and grandfather
before him had left their mark on the criminal ele-
ments of their beloved city.

When he graduated from the police academy, Ski's
first assignment had been with Mike, an officer who'd
turned down multiple offers of promotions to stay on
the street, where he could see what was going on and
what was being done about it. His frequent storms of
protests were legion; if he saw an injustice, he made it
known to his captain, the police chief and the commissioner. Mike never backed away from appearing in
court for his cases even when his life was threatened
by those he charged.

The law degree he'd earned through the years was
used against the lawyers who tended to throw their
weight around when it came to policemen of the

street. Sergeant Gresham's dissatisfaction at such practices was immediately evident, and most of them had learned to tread softly when he was the arresting officer.

It was beginner's luck that threw Ski together with the nine-year veteran out of all the men in the department, and for three years every day had been one to remember, a lesson in itself.

Ski studied the darkly handsome face now as Mike bent over their report sheet. He was never talkative, but lately it seemed to Ski that he was quieter than ever.

"Who was the old man with Joy? Her father?"

Mike took his time answering, and when he looked across at Ski, he was frowning. "I don't know who he was. Joy's never mentioned having any family."

He regretted snubbing her when she smiled at him, and the realization that he was jealous of the man with her came as a shock. It wasn't her boss; he'd met Tom Conan. He knew so little about Joy; he'd never let himself be curious about her.

His thoughts found their way without trouble back to Saturday night when he held her as she cried over another man. Once Joy had told him she couldn't exist without love, and she found it hard to come to terms with a life empty of that emotion. He moved in the seat as he recalled how the night ended, making love to her as he'd wanted to for so long. She was soft and warm and vulnerable, and he couldn't let her go until she belonged to him.

The shift ended, and at precinct headquarters he

picked up his car and said good night to Ski, who planned to pick Paula up when she got off work. Somewhere between the station and the street he should have taken to go home, he turned toward Joy's apartment.

Maybe she needed someone to talk to—if he could manage to talk to her instead of holding her as he wanted to do. The first thing he'd do would be to convince her to let him do just that.

The small blue car was in its usual place, but there were no windows on the front side of her apartment, and he couldn't be sure she was there. Without warning he was preoccupied with the things he didn't know about her: What time did she go to bed? What time did she usually get up? Was she hard to wake in the morning? On Saturday she was the one who had awakened first, before daylight. His body tightened at the memory of Joy's body curved against him, the knit shirt rolled up so that most of that body was naked.

Drawing in his breath, he knocked on the door with the small brass "6A" on it. He waited a moment, looking around the shadowy hall, only a small light at the exit door lighting the dimness.

He raised his fist to knock again and heard her voice inquiring, "Who is it?"

"It's Mike, Joy." He waited for what seemed like several minutes before he saw the knob turn slowly and the door swing open. Unsmiling, she stood looking at him, then turned loose of the door.

"Come in, Mike." He thought the invitation was reluctant, to say the least.

Backing away for a few feet, she stopped and waited for him to speak. He asked the first rational question he could come up with. "Are you all right?"

She nodded and moved to the hassock and sat down, watching him with unblinking eyes all the while. She was dressed the way she must have gone to work, a peach-colored linen dress with square neckline trimmed in narrow white braid. Even the A-line shape of the material did nothing to hide the curves of her breast and gentle roundness of her hips.

He crossed to her and sat down on the floor close enough to touch her. "I haven't stopped thinking about you since Saturday," he said, knowing it was true. Not since Saturday, Sunday, Monday...she hadn't been far from his thoughts at any given hour lately.

She looked at him, still without speaking, her eyes roaming over his face to the open neck of the white civilian shirt he wore. He, in turn, looked her over. The shadows were still beneath her eyes, but the hurt was gone from the blue depths, replaced by another look. Acceptance, he thought. *She's finally accepted the fact that Ken is no longer hers.* A thrill of delight went through him. She was on her way to being on her own again without depending on someone else to always be there.

"Who was the man with you at the coffee shop?" he asked.

"Dan Corvair from Washington, D.C."

He frowned at her short answer. "Part of your family?"

"No." She rubbed her arms and his eyes went to her left hand with its bare ring finger.

He waited but she offered no other explanation as to who Dan Corvair was. Standing up, he reached to pull her into his arms, holding her close as she stiffened against him.

His fingers went over her hair and came back to lift her chin so that she was forced to look up at him. "Joy," he said, "I told you I was sorry, honey, but I'm not. Not sorry about us." He bent to place his mouth on hers and felt the tremor pass through her body. He drew her with him to the couch and sat down, still holding her. She lay against him, her right hand resting on his thigh, her left one on his belt at his waistline.

After a long time while they sat quietly, she stirred. "Would you like something to drink?"

"Like what?"

She sat up and looked at him. "All I have is Coke or coffee." She gave a small shrug. "You choose."

He couldn't think of anything he wanted more than to hold her. "No. Come back here." He motioned to his shoulder, but she stood up and moved away from him.

"We're too different, aren't we, Mike? You conduct your relationships on the short-term basis, where I look for permanency. I can't help it; that's the way I'm built. We can't all be strong like you; I'm not sure I even want to be. I want to worry over someone and have him worry over me. Maybe wonder if I'll get to live my life out to old age, or if it will be shortened by some of your hated criminals. Life's a gamble, Mike; you gamble with yours every day while you protect me.'' She laughed a little. "Don't belittle my borrowing someone else's philosophy when I say build your roads on today because tomorrow's ground is too uncertain for plans.'' She went into the kitchen and put coffee in the coffee maker.

He watched her movements in the small kitchen area. She stood straight, the slim shoulders no longer showing uncertainty. She was fighting back at whatever life had thrown her, and chances were she'd be all right on her own.

"Don't make coffee for me, Joy. I'll take a rain check." She looked around as he got to the door. "Good night, Joy," he said.

It was dark as he drove home, the lights over the city turning the night into daylight brightness as tourists and casinos got together for another round of trying to outguess each other. His thoughts were not on the city or its problems as they usually were even when he was off duty. They were on the woman in the small apartment behind him, a woman who had found strength she didn't know she possessed.

JOY HAD NEVER FOUND the time to line up her vacation to coincide with a trip to Red Lodge, but instead Tom sent her to New York and on up into Montreal. The representatives of the firm there gave her a tour of their bustling city, and she tried out some of her college French on the local shops. Laughing over her failings, she reverted completely to English to buy what she wanted and found the natives spoke better English than she did. Besides that, the tourists from several countries, including the United States, used their mix-and-match languages wherever they went, and effectively at that.

She arrived home on the Fourth of July weekend. In the airport she idly watched crowds of milling tourists as she waited for her baggage.

"Coming or going?" a familiar voice asked, and she turned to face Paula.

"Just getting home. How about you?"

"Ski and Mike are coming in from Denver. Mike's mother invited them up for a few days to loaf and relax and stuff." Paula looked her over. "Where were you this time?"

Joy described her visit, which had extended from the original week scheduled to ten days. "I'd never been up into Canada before, so Tom obligingly sent me up there. From Maine on up through the islands on the Canadian side. It's quite different, with a really primitive coastline, and beautiful."

Paula sighed. "Must be nice to work for people who pay for all these fabulous trips."

Joy agreed. "It is." She wanted to ask if anyone had missed her but immediately gave up the idea.

Baggage started circling around on the conveyor belt, and Joy turned to watch for hers. "What flight are you meeting?" she asked Paula.

"Due in fifteen minutes. Want to wait with me?"

She spotted her bag and pulled it off the belt, shaking her head. "I have to report in to the boss; he's expecting me to call." Smiling, she added, "Give Ski and Mike my best."

Back in her apartment, she placed her call to Tom without stopping to unpack and, a few minutes later, sighed as she undressed and got ready for bed. Tom was happy with her report, and she was tired without really having done any hard work to account for it.

On Saturday the Conan building was deserted as Joy pulled into her usual parking place before eight o'clock. Anyone noticing the slim figure hurry into the building wouldn't have thought she was one of the young executives of Conan Enterprises. She wore tan riding breeches and an open-necked tan-and-blue short-sleeved shirt, and carried a fat briefcase. Through the deserted hallways into her own office, she moved without hesitation and was soon seated at the computer, pushing buttons and turning switches to get on the terminal she wanted to use.

Having awakened sometime during the previous night, she'd decided that if she could program dams and other complicated projects, surely she could do something about the mess her life was in with that smart little machine. She'd just program a little happiness, a bit of strength, a lot of wisdom and mix well.

For two hours Joy sat engrossed in the outlines and figures she punched into the sleek mechanical miracle in front of her. When she finally pushed her chair back and rubbed her stiff neck muscles, she flipped the switch of the printer and watched, fascinated, as the paper rolled up in front of her. It finished running and clicked off, and she tore the printed page away,

folded it without looking at it and put it in her briefcase, locking the door behind her as she left, still without seeing another person. In her car she sat for a
moment and then shook her head and grinned as she
pulled from the parking area and headed for the riding
stables at the park on the opposite side of town.

She rode the gentle red-brown gelding, her mind
blank of any treacherous thoughts, returned the horse
to the stables and, ravenously hungry, went to get a
late lunch in a small restaurant on an out-of-the-way
street.

As her eyes became accustomed to the dimness inside, she ordered and then looked around at the few
people eating in the slow business hours of midafter-
noon. She was almost finished eating when she
looked up at diners being seated a few tables from her.
Her breath caught and she felt the color drain from
her face as her hands gripped her napkin.

Ken, Penny and a young woman were smiling and
talking to one another like very old friends. She
watched them, Penny leaning toward Ken and talking, then turning to the girl, smiling shyly. The young
woman was pretty in a girl-next-door kind of way, but
animation made her features light up as Ken hung on
her every word.

Joy picked up her ticket and walked along the back
area of the dining room to the cashier, keeping her
face turned away from the others. It wouldn't have
mattered; the occupants of the table had eyes for no
one but themselves.

Outside, she stood with her hand on the door

handle of her car, surprised that the sight of Ken with someone else didn't hurt at all. Regret stirred inside and that was all. Regret that she didn't have the ability to cope with a haunted marriage. Regret that she had never gained Penny's love; regret at losing the baby.

She couldn't blame her youth—she wasn't that young when she married Ken. At twenty-six, she'd had plenty of experience with children at the orphanage, the different personalities and how to handle them, how to coax the most unhappy ones to smile once in a while. Her job at Conan Enterprises had taken her into hundreds of different situations, many of them difficult. And not all the people she dealt with were easy to get along with, but she managed.

She wondered what the printout in her briefcase would show. What had the computer determined was her status in life? Suddenly she knew she would manage without the conclusions derived from the sassy little machine she manipulated every day to give her answers to complicated problems in the world of business.

I'll win, she thought, and knew it was true. Joy could do it all alone—it would be hard, but possible. She stood there, feeling the uncertainty inside her dissolve and a new feeling of determination taking its place. Traffic moved on the street; the car in front of hers pulled away from the curb and another parked in its place, and still she stood there. From this day, her life was her own again.

"Joy?" The voice was nearby, and she came back from a great distance to look up at Mike getting out of the patrol car that had pulled into the space in front of her.

"Hello, Mike," she said and waved to Ski, who was driving.

Mike stopped beside her, looking down at her hand holding tightly to the door of her car. "How have you been?"

"All right." Her eyes strayed to the briefcase on the car seat and back to Mike.

He looked uncertain for a moment. "Paula and Maude are having a cookout at their house tomorrow. They'd like you to come." When she didn't answer immediately, he went on, "I was planning to call you tonight."

"Yes, Mike. Would you tell Paula I'd love to come? What about bringing something with me?"

He shook his head. "We have everything all set up, with plenty to eat. About two o'clock?"

She nodded. He didn't move, and she looked up to find dark gray eyes going over her neatly attired figure in trim riding pants. "Are you doing all right otherwise, Joy?"

"Yes." Sure, she was doing all right, otherwise. Whatever that meant.

"I get off at eight tonight. Can I come by to see you?"

She was careful to make sure that her indrawn breath wasn't audible. "I already have plans, Mike." Getting her life back together didn't include letting her uncontrollable emotions dictate to her. Where Mike was concerned, she had to watch her step.

"Okay," he said, turning back to the patrol car. "We'll see you tomorrow."

The car pulled away, and she got into hers, driving across town in heavy traffic. Tourists intent on seeing all there was to see; checking out the gambling joints they planned to visit that evening. Just off North Virginia Avenue, she glanced at the saddle-shaped roof of the atmospheric planetarium. It boasted a one-hundred-and-eighty-degree motion picture projector that recreated atmospheric phenomena, changing programs about every three minutes. She hadn't been there in a long time, but now she could start back to attending all the new programs, since most of her evenings would be free.

At home, she put her briefcase in the small closet by the front door and ignored the papers she'd spent so much care in preparing. In her quest to program her life into some semblance of order, she'd forgotten the human angle, as was so easy with a computer. The machine was a whiz, but its heart hadn't been developed to its full sensitivity yet.

Maybe I'll get a patent on one for that purpose and be a millionaire while helping the lonely and brokenhearted. A most noble aspiration, she concluded.

Chapter Sixteen

Sunday dawned clear and bright, a typical summer day for Reno, with a few puffs of clouds within Joy's view as she walked to get her morning paper. The streets were already teeming with crowds on their way to Fourth of July celebrations. The bigger parades had been on Saturday, while she'd sat in front of the little machine at Conan's and played with numbers, cursors, binaries and modems—while lines intersected and divided and told her she was having a great time and her life was all settled to her satisfaction. That would teach her to believe what a human being derived from punching information into such a mechanical vehicle. She smiled to herself and saw the lines on printed paper as she ripped them to shreds and threw them in the garbage. It had given her something to do with an otherwise empty Saturday morning. Her nose wrinkled just for an instant and she shrugged. Joy wasn't usually one to waste time like that, but she supposed it had served its purpose.

Her steps moved faster, and she took her paper,

making a circle of the one block she was on, and headed for the apartment. She spread the front page out, scanning the columns for anything unusual in the way of news. Not much had changed from last weekend.

It was almost two o'clock when she stepped into her car, dressed in navy-blue shorts, a red-and-white-striped polo shirt and red thong sandals, a wide red band holding her hair away from her face, making her look somewhat like a walking Uncle Sam advertisement. She was sentimentally patriotic and didn't mind at all. At Paula's, she pulled in behind Ski's car and reached into the backseat for the two big milk jugs she'd filled with lemonade.

"Need help?"

She turned, smiling at Mike. "Yes," she said, handing him the jugs.

Without talking, they walked around the side of the small bungalow and were greeted by choruses from Ski, Paula and Maude. As Mike turned away to put the lemonade on the long redwood table, Joy took in his slim tight-muscled body in jeans and light blue knit shirt opened at the throat.

Her eyes were still on him when he turned to look at her. "I built the fire; it's up to them to cook. Come on, Joy, let's play horseshoes."

It had been years since she'd held one of the heavy iron shoes, but she liked the game. Swinging her arms to limber them, she watched Mike throw a ringer the first time and shook her head.

"I'm out of my league," she told him.

He grinned and said so that only she could hear, "A kiss for each game you lose."

Her gaze locked with his and he was no longer smiling. She bit her lip and turned to measure the distance between the two stakes. She threw the horseshoe and it landed on the point, tumbling three feet away from where she intended it to go.

He whistled. "You need practice," he said, and proceeded to give her pointers, but he beat her every game, teasing her as they ate and talked about every other subject under the sun. She watched his hands as he squeezed ketchup on a hot dog and remembered the response her body gave to his touch.

If I've learned anything, she thought, *it's that Mike had best be the first word removed from a new vocabulary unless I'm not particular how soon I get outdistanced again.* She was quiet as she helped with the cleanup, listening to the conversation around her.

Mike and Ski were discussing the new class of recruits that would be coming in the first of August and whether they should break up their team and each of them take a new officer temporarily.

"Champion probably won't give us a choice," Ski said, referring to their captain. "He wants you to be the one who takes the newcomers in hand, Mike, and you can't blame him for that."

Mike shook his head. "Look, Ski, you can train them as well as I can. I'd rather we gave the classes and let Rose and Jansen take care of the foot patrols."

Ski grinned. "I'm for that."

It was getting dark and everyone sat, lazing around.

Joy held a paper cup of lemonade for the sole purpose of giving her hands something to do. She was restless, and as Paula moved around straightening things and stacking plates, she joined her.

As soon as everything was put away, she said, "I have a long week ahead of me, Paula, and a lot of preparations to make. Thanks a lot. Next time, the entertainment's on me." She laughed. "Of course, we'll have to go to the mountains or beach; my little hole in the wall isn't big enough to hold all of us."

"Would you drop me off at my place, Joy? Ski isn't ready to leave just yet." Mike spoke from behind her.

She looked around. "Of course, Mike." She bit her lip, wishing she could get out of it gracefully. Being close to Mike still presented a problem for her, as unsure as she was of her ability to hide her feelings.

Mike didn't talk as she turned her car away from Paula's drive and in the direction of the townhouse she'd visited a long time ago. As she pulled into the driveway, she turned to look at him.

"You owe me three kisses," he said quietly. "Come inside with me."

She shook her head. "No, Mike."

"You're reneging on your debt?"

"Some other time," she sat stiffly, waiting for him to get out.

"No." He got out opposite her and came around to open her door. He held out his hand to her, and after a moment's hesitation, she slid out of the car. Silently she walked with him through the front entrance and into the lovely room she remembered from the night she had stayed there, sleeping in his pajamas.

He turned her around to face him, and his hands slid up her arms to fit over her shoulders, lifting her a little as he bent to place his mouth on hers. Standing still, she waited as his lips quietly went over hers, his breath warming her skin.

"It's much more satisfactory if two play the game," he said, looking down into her half-closed eyes.

"I'm not sure of the rules," she whispered.

He smiled. "We'll make them as we go along." He turned her, and she was pulled down on the couch beside him and, as he leaned backward, he took her body with him to lie in his arms. She lowered her face to his.

For a long time, they half lay there, lips touching occasionally, their breath mingling. His hands, loosely clasped behind her across her back, moved downward to press her hips closer, allowing her to feel the desire she aroused in him.

She shook her head and sat up, pushing his hands away from her. "I have to go, Mike."

"I counted only one kiss," he said.

"Let me go."

He stood up and reached down to lift her, striding into his bedroom. The hair on his arms under her legs somehow made his touch more intimate, and she struggled as he put her down on the bed. His hand pressed lightly on her bare thigh the brief shorts made no attempt at covering.

"Stop it, Joy," he said, sitting beside her, leaning

toward her with his left arm supporting him. "You want me as much as I want you."

She stopped her protests to look into gray eyes dark with the feelings he didn't try to hide. This, then, was what Mike wanted. She was a divorcée, fair game for a man who needed female companionship only for temporary purposes. It didn't matter to him she'd lost a love and, in the process of recuperation, replaced it with one she thought would be solid. Not that she really pretended it would be returned, but she thought Mike would be, at the least, sympathetic. Not strong enough to be a wife for him, she would be a substitute for a while, according to all the laws of nature between male and female.

Rain on you, Mike Gresham, she thought fiercely and shoved, catching Mike by surprise. At the door she whirled, eyes shooting blue sparks at the handsome man watching her. Her hands clenched.

"Yes, Mike, I want you. That you expected, but let me add something you don't want to hear." Her breath was loud in the room. "My wanting is accompanied by another emotion you refuse to recognize. I may not be as strong as you think a woman should be, but my love could outlast any fear I might have for whatever the new day brings.'

She turned to the open bedroom door and flung over her shoulder: "Don't worry, Mike. I won't embarrass you with my feelings, and I'll stay out of your territory. I'll be gone most of the summer, so you won't have to worry about running into me."

"Where's Conan sending you now?"

"He isn't sending; I volunteered. Next week I'll be in Lake Tahoe and in Indianapolis the following week. After that I'll try Montana to see if that's far enough away from you." She caught the doorknob. "Goodbye, Mike." She slammed the door and ran, grabbing her billfold and keys as she went by the table.

The hurt was too deep for tears, and she drove without seeing any of the beautiful homes and yards on Mike's side of town. The emptiness inside of her was remindful of the long, narrow halls at the orphanage when one of the children had been adopted. She always missed the ones that left and secretly cried herself to sleep many nights when a favorite was fortunate enough to be able to claim parents and a home of his own, ashamed of the jealousy she couldn't express or let anyone see. Once again she was fourteen, and the loss today was doubled to go with her twenty-eight years.

When she reached her apartment the phone was ringing, but she threw herself across the middle of the bed, oblivious to the persistent noise. If it was Tom Conan, he'd see her tomorrow; anyone else could forget it.

SHE NEVER TIRED of the Lake Tahoe area. It was out of her reach as a way of life, but she nevertheless enjoyed being there. The lake itself was a sparkling blue jewel surrounded by the towering peaks of the Sierra Nevada. She often wondered what the first settlers to arrive in this wilderness had thought when they saw it for the first time.

The clients on her schedule were mostly men, some of whom thought a lovely young woman turned loose in their world was there for the express purpose of finding a husband or, better yet, a temporary lover. She fielded the passes, discussed the business with serious determination, and felt a sense of success when she saw realization in their eyes that she knew what she was talking about and was interested first and foremost in the job.

Tom Conan had taught her well, and he would have been the first to put the male predators in their places. He knew it happened, but he had faith in her that she could handle the few who tried to take advantage of her. She didn't let him down, never giving in to the anger that sometimes intruded no matter how much she tried not to let it get to her.

Her client on Friday was one of her favorites, Carlton Ridenhour, of the famous—or infamous—Ridenhours. Racehorses, race cars, shipping lines—you name it, and he had a few billion dollars tied up in the business. The luncheon he gave at his palatial estate above the clear waters of Lake Tahoe was a studied piece of understatement.

One of the dignified waiters stopped near her with a tray. She smiled at him, her dimples flashing, and he returned the smile, something he was not really accustomed to doing, she thought.

Studying the assortment of dainty sandwiches, nuts, cheeses and fruits, Joy selected two of the sandwiches and a slice of fresh pineapple and moved out of his path so that he could circle the huge room. She sat alone on a

marble window seat, watching the crowd of business-
men, playboys and their ladies.

"I knew I gave the contract to the right outfit,"
Carlton Ridenhour told her as he sat on the edge of
the seat near her.

"Of course," she agreed, letting her pride show.
"Mr. Conan is the best one anytime you have such an
undertaking."

He shook his head. "That isn't what I meant." He
looked around the room in the same way as she had,
as though seeing the group for the first time. "Tom
sends a lovely woman who has brains." He smiled at
her. "She does business when it's time to do business
and eats when it's time to eat. I like that." He watched
her take the last bite of her sandwich. "Ever think of
leaving Conan's?"

Startled, she lifted her gaze to meet the dark seri-
ousness of his. "No."

She really never had; Tom Conan was family to her
whether he thought of her that way or not. Long ago
he had become very important to her as her friend
and as her boss, and she would never voluntarily
leave him.

"I'm serious," he went on. "We're moving the
new planning unit for the shipping line from San Di-
ego to Sacramento. I'd like to put you in charge of the
marketing operation."

She shook her head and smiled. "Thank you, Mr.
Ridenhour. It's a pleasure to do business with you,
and I appreciate the compliment, but..." She let the
sentence drop as someone came to claim his attention.

He rose to go, looking down at her from his short height. "Think about it, Joy. I'll talk to you and Tom next week."

As she made her way through the club-sized rooms to the outside, she thought about the offer and discarded it. The salary would be fabulous, but she would be lost in the giant conglomerate that made up the vast fortunes commanded by the Ridenhours.

Smiling to herself, she got into her car and headed for home. Next week would be a new experience, since Tom was sending her to Indianapolis, where she'd never been. Originally he'd planned to go himself but decided he was needed in Red Lodge to check the extensive revisions of the dam plans there. When the changes were done to satisfy him, she would have another computer program to work out, and by that time the summer would be over. She sighed as she turned into the driveway of her apartment building, unsure of whether she was glad or sorry that time sailed so hurriedly by her.

The phone was ringing as she threw her handbag on the couch, and she kicked off her white high-heeled sandals as she reached for it.

"Hello?"

"Joy, it's Mike."

Her body stiffened and she bit hard into her lower lip. Somehow Joy had convinced herself that Mike would be finished with her after their last encounter and would go look for a strong lady who could endure with him. Her fight to keep from feeling vulnerable and weak was beginning to seem like a losing battle where Mike was concerned.

"Yes, Mike?" Her head lifted and soft lips settled into a firm line.

"I've been trying to reach you for a couple of days and finally called your office. Mr. Conan said you were in Tahoe, and he expected you home today."

"Yes, I just came in the door."

"Tired?"

The quick thoughtful question drew her up short as she prepared to light into him should he mention her debt of kisses she still owed him.

"No," she answered, "I'm not tired." She smiled a little as she remembered what she'd done to earn her salary the past few days. Signed a glorious contract for her boss, ate like a construction worker, and turned down the offer of a glamorous job, whether it was a serious offer or not.

She felt his hesitation. "We're on duty tonight, but I'll be free after four tomorrow afternoon. Would you like to go swimming?"

No, Mike, she wanted to say. *I don't want to go anywhere with you. I don't want to expose myself to anything more I can't handle.* "I'd love to go, Mike. Where?"

She heard his indrawn breath before he answered. Mike wasn't all that sure of himself either, perhaps. "I know a beautiful beach not far from here. It's private, so it won't be very crowded."

"Private?" She had a sudden vision of the two of them alone far from any other people. That was something she didn't want.

He laughed. "Not that private," he said, as though

reading her mind. "A dozen or so families use it, but I meant not crowded like the public beaches."

"Okay, Mike," she said. "What time?"

"Pick you up at five o'clock?"

"Yes. I'll be ready."

MIKE WAS RIGHT—the beach had several people wandering around on it and a few more in the water, but it wasn't crowded. He carried a picnic basket and a blanket rolled up under his arm, stopping under a huge orange-and-white-striped umbrella with a table and two chairs.

"Just for us?"

"Reserved with forethought."

She helped him spread the food from the basket. "I assume Maude had a little to do with this?"

"Right."

In the short time she'd been in the small circle of friends, she knew that Maude in particular looked out for both the men when it came to extra preparations of food.

"Figures," she said now. "I'm hungry."

Surprised, she found it was true. After Mike had called her Friday night, she talked to Tom, did whatever required doing to the apartment, went into the office on Saturday morning without eating breakfast, and had a fast slice of pizza brought in at noon by one of the men working along with her, and that was all. She had barely had time to change into pale yellow shorts and shirt and find her bathing suit before Mike knocked on her door.

They sat near each other, eyes narrowed against the glare of the late-afternoon sun on the smooth lake surface. After they finished eating, Mike spread the blanket and they lay down, not talking. He turned to her, his arm going across her, pushing her arm from her face where she had covered her eyes. Long fingers touched her cheek, turning her to face him, and his mouth was firm and cool as it touched hers.

Closing her eyes, she waited for him to finish the kiss and move away, but he didn't finish. Pressure from his mouth increased, and he forced her lips apart to slip his tongue inside and quickly withdraw it, taking his time to go around her mouth, to her cheek, nibbling to her earlobe, downward to the pulse in her throat. His breath came quickly, and she clenched her fists to keep from reaching to hold him close.

He raised his head to look down at her. "You're fighting me," he said. "Stop it."

"We've waited long enough to go swimming," she said, looking straight up at him.

After a moment of deep eye contact, he sat up, pulling her with him. "You can change there." He pointed to a bright green-and-white cabana, and she took her suit and towel without a word and walked away from him. She was shaking.

He was coming from opposite her as she finished dressing, and she stepped out to meet him. He said nothing as his eyes went over her slim figure, rounded breasts pushing at the shirred top of her one-piece bathing suit, a deep purple with tiny white sprigs throughout. The color turned her eyes to deep violet and accented her creamy skin against the jet black of her hair.

Her breath caught at the sight of Mike's tanned body, a physique she knew by touch, intensely remembered against her own slender form. Tearing her gaze away, she pushed the heavy hair under her swim cap. He took her hand, and they ran down to the water, diving together into the coolness, swimming for several seconds before he let up and waited for her.

"Let's go for the float."

"Okay." They swam a few more yards, and he pulled her up to sit with him, their feet splashing in the water.

"I go on duty tomorrow at three, but we could have breakfast with Grace before I go," he said after a few minutes of silence.

For a moment she continued to look out over the rippling lake surface before she turned to smile at him. "Is there a chance of snow?"

"Not one," he promised.

"If you're really sure, I'll go."

He took her hand, and they slid into the water swimming with long, even strokes back to the sandy shoreline. She refused to think of the feelings left inside her from his kisses, wondering how to avoid further torture. The soft, melting sweetness that his touch transmitted to her was best kept hidden from Mike. If he ever suspected how she felt, all her best arguments would be less than useless, and he would have her exactly where he wanted her. She wasn't helping her own cause by agreeing to go anywhere and everywhere he invited her. But their times together would be few and far between, what with his long hours and her frequent travels. Certainly, she could hold together for a few hours without betraying her growing feelings for Mike.

As they sat on the blanket, towels across their shoulders, she asked, "Where are Paula and Ski today?"

"They're in Carson City visiting her parents."

She turned to look at him. "When I saw Paula at the airport last weekend, she said you and Ski had been to see your mother in Denver. Does she ever come out here?"

"She was here at Christmas."

Her gaze met his, and she turned to look out over the water. Christmas, when Mike had bought her hot chocolate and eaten cookies with her. Christmas, when Mike kissed her for the first time. Christmas, a long, long time ago.

Her breath was unsteady, but she worked until she couldn't hear it very much. Her path was far from downhill, but it was getting easier to think about the past without it being painful.

"Joy."

She didn't look at him but stiffened when he touched her arm. He pushed her backward on the blanket, pulling the towel from her shoulders to place it beside her. His wide shoulders between her and the setting sun shadowed her face, and she couldn't see the expression in his eyes. She didn't have to; whatever he was feeling was answered by her traitorous heart and body. Her lips parted before his mouth descended on hers, and she made a small sound as his body partly covered hers, his wanting her evident in the hardness of the body pressed into hers.

"Sweet," he whispered, his mouth barely on hers. "Joy?"

Her eyes flew wide as he drew in a deep breath and lay beside her, cradling her head on the hard muscle of his left arm, his right one across her middle, his lips on the tender nerve just below her ear. She shivered and his arm tightened, but he said nothing more, his arms unrelenting as he pulled her closer and closer.

Chapter Seventeen

It was getting dark when Joy stirred. "How late does the beach stay open?" A sign she'd read earlier said there were restricted hours for the private man-made beach.

Mike didn't move. "We can go to my place."

They remained in that position for several minutes until he sat up, pulling her with him, and they began to pull on their clothes and gather the picnic items to put into the trunk of his car. Still without speaking, he shook the blanket they'd been lying on and put it in the trunk beside the basket, turning to help her into the car. He glanced at her as he slid into the seat opposite her.

"It would be better if you take me home, Mike," she said, her voice tight.

He didn't answer her, and as they entered the city limits, he turned the car toward his side of town. She looked away from him out the window over the city where the lights made a carpet of pale yellow below them as they topped a slight ridge.

Silently they unloaded the car in the garage and

took their picnic paraphernalia with them into the kitchen. Her glance appreciated the sparkling spacious townhouse Mike said belonged to his mother. She'd never had a mother—would Mike's object to his bringing her there to make love to her? Did she know how many others had been there before her?

You could have stopped him from bringing you here, Joy, she admonished herself, *if you'd had any desire to do so.* Her desire lay in a different direction, and it was too late to run.

Mike's hands on her arms turned her to face him, and she opened her mouth to tell him she must go; but his lips covered hers effectively, stopping anything she might have said.

The thin knit of her shirt allowed his hands to transmit their feelings into her body, and she leaned against him as his fingers moved over the firm mounds of her breasts to her waist. One hand came back to tangle in her hair, the other cupping her hip to hold her ever closer to him.

He raised his head to look down at her, and Joy slowly opened her eyes. Bending a little, he picked her up without much effort, carrying her to his bedroom. He stood her on her feet and reached to pull the shirt over her head. She was still, looking into his dark eyes, then put her hand to his shirt front, unbuttoning the buttons, concentrating to keep her mind from telling her she could still stop her straight path to destruction.

He finished undressing her, and she waited as his eyes went over her figure. Breasts that were full but small enough to go with the slender waist, rounded hips and firm thighs. He pushed her backward until she sat on the bed.

"Move over," he said quietly, and as she did so, he finished removing his own clothing and lay beside her.

He brought her close to him, and they lay a long time before she felt him tremble, and he whispered, "Joy." She slid her hand along his hip, hesitating, and made a quick move to withdraw from his arms, but he held her. "No, darling. You can't leave me now."

His mouth sought hers, and finding the warm moistness of her lips, he kissed softly, murmuring love words to her. Her heart listened and answered even as her mind fought for reasoning. Her mind lost the battle and her lips parted as she responded, biting into his full lower lip, bringing her leg up between his as she sought to get closer to him.

His quick intake of breath lighted the fires smoldering inside her, and her lips left his to travel down over his chin to his throat, across his chest. She bit gently into the hard nipple before moving across his ribs to his stomach. He held her head to him until, with a groan, he pulled her back up into his arms, wrapping her slight body with his.

With slow caressing movements, his hand went from her flat belly down to her thighs, pulling gently to separate them. He looked down into her wide-open eyes, smiling as he kissed them closed, lifting her hips as he entered her.

Suspended in the silvery cloud of awareness that she now belonged to Mike, she responded to his movements with slow reflexes, bringing her legs around him to keep him inside her. For a few seconds they were able to hold back, but then she clasped him to her and her breath jarred through her body as the soul-shattering result of their lovemaking shook them. He moved quickly, and suddenly the world exploded for them as he held her to him, moaning with the unbearable ecstasy. There was no need to talk; for the moment she believed what his arms and lips told her. They lay in each other's arms without moving.

IT SEEMED ONLY AN INSTANT until the jangling ring of the telephone intruded into her sleep, and Joy struggled to reach it, but she was held firmly in Mike's arms. He leaned across her to pick up the receiver, listening for a moment.

"All right," he said. "Give me thirty minutes, and I'll meet you at headquarters." He replaced the receiver and lay back on the pillow, all without releasing her from his arms. Her body rested in the curve of his, her head pillowed on one arm. The room was dark, and she stared into the dimness, waiting for him to speak.

When he didn't, she put her hand over his where it rested on her breast. "What is it?"

"I have to go to work." His arm tightened around her. "Can we take a rain check on the breakfast?"

She thought about it. "The snowstorm was probably safer than this."

"Yes," he agreed. After a moment, he said, "I have to go, sweetheart."

She turned on her back, still within the circle of his arms. "I know."

He kissed her cheek and pulled his arm from beneath her, touching her lips with long fingers. "Go back to sleep."

She listened to him moving around and dressing, and when he finished, he came back to sit on the edge of the bed. He had turned on the light in the living room, and there was enough light coming through the doorway so that she could see his face. His eyes followed the movement of his hand as he smoothed the tumbled black hair from her cheek. He smiled as his hand moved over her bare shoulder to caress the smooth skin exposed there.

"I wish I didn't have to go," he whispered and bent to kiss her.

She wanted to hold him to her, and suddenly she knew what he meant when he said a woman must be stronger than her policeman husband. If she had the right, she'd lie there and worry about him until he came home or called to tell her he was all right. If she had the right, and were strong enough, she would worry, but she'd go about her daily routine until he was back in her arms again.

He straightened and stood up, squeezing her hand before he let go. "I'll call you. Will you be here or at home?"

"I'll call a cab and go home."

But Mike didn't call, and she was afraid to call the station to ask what had happened to get him back on duty in the middle of the night. A problem that went on into the morning when he was supposedly off duty; one that went on into the day and through Sunday night as well, since she didn't hear anything from him. Or maybe she wouldn't hear from him again. Without the right to worry, she did it, anyway.

MIKE WASN'T usually so impatient with meetings that brought as many changes as this one promised to do. Most of it centered around him, and he was forced to listen, to agree or disagree, to argue, to explain. Across the room, his eyes met Ski's, and his partner nodded.

The discussion went on, and Mike's thoughts wandered back to the bed where he'd left Joy. A delicious thrill went through him, straightening him in the chair, as he allowed himself a brief moment to recapture the sweetness of the previous day and night. She was his. She had given herself to him without reservations; her thoughts, her entire being had been given to him as she lay in his arms, loving him as completely as he loved her.

"Well, that effectively postpones the rest of these assignments," Captain Champion was saying, and Mike's attention swung back to the room. He didn't know what was postponing what. Shaking away the stirring thoughts of Joy, he looked up as Ski stopped beside him.

"Let's go, Mike. They have our car ready and waiting."

Ski would have to fill him in on whatever was happening. Never in twelve years of police work had his partner had to do that. He had known Joy Strayer was going to bring some changes into his life; he was beginning to realize just how much she might change it.

Chapter Eighteen

Joy's gaze rested unseeingly on the traffic as the cab-driver threaded his way through downtown India-napolis. During the flight, she'd kept her mind busy going over the strenuous schedule she had to follow the next four days, ending with a big luncheon planned for everyone on Saturday afternoon. It would be late Saturday night before she got back to Reno, but it didn't matter. No one was worrying about whether she returned or not; unless Tom did. And even he had told her not to bother calling when she got in; the information she gathered could wait till Sunday morning.

Her mind sought its wayward path back to Mike. It seemed never to tire of doing everything contrary to her wishes, forcing her to think about things she'd rather not, where she seemed unable to make rational decisions.

Nothing had changed for Mike, but her world, which she thought was in some semblance of order, collapsed around her again with the realization she loved the policeman who regarded her as a pretty plaything, too soft and afraid to endure a life with him. It wasn't as if he'd led her on—he told her enough times what was required of policemen's wives and of his belief that such women didn't exist. He was right; it would take a unique person to stay home and wait out the uncertainty.

I must do something about the erratic pattern of my life, she decided, and shook her shoulders as the cab drew up in front of the hotel. She stared out at the imposing structure, a multistory building that seemed to stretch forever into the dark sky.

Inside the ultraplush lobby, she signed for the room Tom had changed to her name and was slightly intimidated by the surroundings as a young man took her bags and moved to the elevators with her. The center of the lobby was a glassed-wall atrium reaching several stories above the luxurious entrance.

The young man smiled at her as he opened the door to her room and placed her bags inside, tipping his elegant blue-and-gold cap as he left her. If the lobby was plush, the rooms were something else—big, the last word in elegance.

Mentally she compared the room with the Yodeler in Red Lodge, remembering that she'd thought it an extravagance, to be used only in the case of a big expense account.

She wouldn't even ask what this had set the company back, she thought, and grinned as she sat on the heavily embossed spread covering a queen-sized bed. Of course, this was originally meant for the boss; she had just lucked out this time.

WITH ALL THE conferences behind them by Friday noon, Mr. LeGrange, president of the Forsyth Company that dealt in raw materials for building contractors, asked that they break for lunch and then work straight through to finish up everything that evening. He had been called to New York and had to leave early Saturday morning.

Joy was glad. They had worked hard, she was tired and ready to go home, realizing more than ever that when Tom went for conferences on his projects, he worked like a Trojan. No wonder he had gone to Red Lodge instead of Indianapolis. However, there was a definite plus in the hard work she had done—it left little time to brood about Mike, and for that she was thankful.

With a glance at her watch, she dialed the airline reservations office and was lucky enough to be able to change her flight from four on Saturday afternoon to the seven o'clock flight that night. It would put her home somewhere around ten, and she could wait until morning to report to Tom, since he wasn't expecting her until the following night. Her reports were all finalized and looked good for the company; she was proud of them and Tom would be, too.

She looked through the thick batch of papers she had worked on through the week of continuous meetings, discussions and decisions. Somehow she felt that few people noticed she was a "mere" woman, and that pleased her enormously. They listened when she made suggestions; when she asked questions or made a comment in answer to an invitation to do so, they

paid attention. Her papers were rough drafts of programs, insurance litigation, accounting procedures
they would have to follow and general engineering
outlines that Tom would work into a readable format.
Her work would go into the computer and, she hoped,
would come out with a multitude of outlines that fit
with the results of Tom's decisions. When all that was
finished, a broad complex of a modern medical
center, a product of Conan Enterprises, would grace
an area now covered by abandoned warehouses, the
result of months of planning and work on their part.

Brushing her hair, she suddenly felt Mike's fingers
running through it, and she stiffened as her body relived the thrill of his touch. She laid the brush down
on the shining surface of the dressing table and went
to the window to look out into the sparkling summer
afternoon. In Reno, three hours behind them here,
Mike and Ski would be looking for a quick sandwich
to eat on the run.

It was almost a week now since Mike held her,
loved her as though he had the right to do so. And not
a word since that time. When he wanted her again,
she supposed he thought she'd be there waiting for
him.

Joy watched the surge of humans on the sidewalk
six stories below her, minute figures bustling in the
sultry July afternoon. She could see the hotel reflected in windows across the street, out of sight
above her head. It was an engineering marvel, an elegant monument to the architects and engineers who
put together the glass and stone to make a breathtak-

ing facade of undefinable luxury. "Intimidating" was an apt description.

Shaking her head to clear it of pensive thoughts, she went to dress, selecting the dark gray voile as her outfit to wear the last day. She had worn it on Wednesday morning, so maybe none of them would remember it was being recycled. The women would, of course, but most of them were in the same boat, able to pack only a few things for dressy affairs. She surveyed the result in the gold-framed mirror; it was a becoming outfit. The white piping gave relief to the gray, bringing out different lights in her eyes.

Rolling her heavy hair into a loose coil off her neck, she fastened combs to hold it where they wouldn't show and pulled a thick tendril in front of each ear where she punched white button-shaped earrings with a gray star in the center. She backed away to see the overall effect and went to get a small handbag she could hold flat against her briefcase and not have to worry about putting down and forgetting it, as she had been known to do. Briefly she thought of Ken's impatience with her when she couldn't find her billfold, her keys, her gloves. Actually he'd always been impatient with her for something or other.

The hurt that came with memories of Ken was gone now. He seldom surfaced in her thoughts, and there was only faint regret for what might have been. Her numerous faults went unnoticed by anyone.

And Mike? He would take her, faults and all, if she weren't so wary of a temporary relationship. *Nothing permanent, you understand, Joy, because you aren't*

*strong enough; you couldn't take being a policeman's
wife, remember? Suppose I were killed? Suppose...*

*Well, Mike, suppose I were killed? Suppose the plane I
get on tonight crashed somewhere in the vastness between
Indianapolis and Reno? Would you be strong? Wouldn't
you cry just a little, Mike? Is that such a weak characteristic that you couldn't even grieve if you lost me? Well,
you never had me, Mike, not so you'd ever have to worry
about being weak if you lost me to a plane crash or a
careless motorist or a gunman.*

I want someone to cry over me when I'm gone, she
thought, *someone to miss me because I'm no longer
there. Nothing is permanent, Mike; even you agree to
that.*

Nudging Mike out of her thoughts, she closed and
locked the door behind her and walked two floors
down the carpeted stairs to where the conference
room was located and turned along the walkway suspended four floors over the lobby. She stopped to
look down into the lush greenery that lined the
atrium. For a dizzying moment, she watched people
move on another walkway below her, then strolled
along, glancing now and then at the art objects placed
on the wall—vases intricately designed in gold figures,
plants that formed a forested background for the inside luxury of the building. It was, indeed, fabulous.

The conference room was in the center of the building, encompassing a quarter of one side. There were
more than fifty representatives of engineering and insurance firms from across the United States, Canada
and Australia.

Constance Avery was with the owner of Corcoran National out of Montreal, and Joy sat next to her, smiling at the older woman she'd spent several enjoyable hours with after some of the meetings, renewing their acquaintance from her first trip to Montreal. Mr. LeGrange appeared promptly at two o'clock, and seconds later they were engrossed in the work that would finish the meeting.

With the round of handshaking, congratulations and thanks that ensued at the conclusion, Joy found her hand enclosed in Otto LeGrange's big work-worn hand.

"Tell Tom my wife and I will be out there around Labor Day. I don't care much about seeing him, but perhaps you'll show us around."

The dimples appeared. "Of course, Mr. LeGrange. We have a lot to show off, but I must admit, nothing like this." She spread her hands at the elegance around them. "We run more to something a little less...less..." She searched for the right word.

He leaned down to whisper, "Pretentious?"

She smiled. "Yes," she whispered back, liking him even more than before.

A few members of the conference made plans for dinner at the hotel and to attend the popular weekly dances that had become a regular feature there, while others did as she had, planning to leave that same evening, depending on flights.

Joy said her good-byes and hurried to her room to pick up her already-packed luggage, call a cab and rush to the airport. She was cutting it short, leaving the hotel just before six with her plane scheduled for departure at seven. Breathless, she checked in at the counter to confirm that her reservations had been changed and that her Saturday flight had been canceled.

On board the plane, she fastened her seat belt and, with a tired sigh, relaxed against the seat. Not as luxurious as her past week's accommodations, but they'd do for her three-hour flight home.

RENO AIRPORT WAS EMPTY by comparison with Indianapolis, and Joy waited patiently until her luggage appeared on the conveyor. It was just plain good to be home, and she was ready for a quiet evening with nothing to clog her mind. The figures she had compiled in the past several days were going to be forgotten until tomorrow when she called Tom to make her report. He should be happy enough with her success to take her to Godfather's Pizza for lunch. She needed some plain food after all the rich offerings she'd indulged in all week. She grinned to herself; Tom wouldn't consider pizza plain fare—not with his ulcer.

Her car was parked in the long-term lot, and she waited again for it to be brought around for her, paying the cashier and getting a receipt so she could put it on her expense account. She was afraid to look at the spread sheet for the past week—the company had taken a beating.

Traffic wasn't bad at ten-thirty on a Friday night, with most of the driving public firmly ensconced behind the blackjack tables or pulling on the metal arms

of machines in various gambling houses or listening
to the famous and near-famous celebrities imported
for their entertainment.

Joy's gaze rested on the darkened buildings along
Virginia Boulevard with its new gas-vapor streetlights
installed for energy-saving purposes. Two policemen
patrolled on foot, watching for potential criminals or
victims.

Mike. Her body quivered instantly at the thought,
and she drew in her breath as she saw the information
arrow for the turn to police headquarters.

She was driving on the inside lane, and without
warning her hands turned the steering wheel to the
left-turn lane and went into the side street, bringing
her to the front of the police headquarters building
within seconds.

It was a new experience for her being in Mike's
domain, and she stood for a moment, uncertainly
reading the signs giving directions to various rooms
and offices. Mike spent little time in the office; what
in the world made her stop by here?

A burly figure rounded the corner of the hallway,
and the uniformed policeman stopped short at the
sight of the young woman standing in the dimly lit
hallway. He gave her figure an all-encompassing
glance and asked, "May I help you?"

The quick smile brought the dimples into view, and
she touched her crooked tooth with her tongue. "Is
Sergeant Gresham on duty tonight?"

"Yes, ma'am," he said and pointed. "Right through
that door."

Oh, goodness! Now what do I do?

Swallowing hard, she followed the direction of his pointing finger and stood for a second on the outside of the partly opened door before she pushed it inward. Conscious of her heart pounding, she looked quickly round the large room, empty except for the two men with their backs to her.

Ski was standing by a desk looking toward the opposite wall. Mike sat a little in front of him, straddling a straight-backed chair facing away from her. Ski half turned to see who had opened the door, and Joy stopped short as he stiffened, his mouth open.

She gulped over the dry tremor in her throat and said, "Hello, Ski, Mike." Her heart thundered in her chest, and she clutched the small bag so tightly it hurt her fingers.

Ski made a strangled sound as he took a step toward her. Mike jerked around, staring at her with dark eyes. After what seemed an eternity, he turned his head to look at the television set they'd been watching and quickly back to her.

Ski's voice came out a rough groan. "Joy!" Her name was an exclamation of disbelief.

She stared from one to the other as they seemed to move in slow motion, and for a moment, fright kept her silent.

"What's the matter?" she asked finally when neither of the men spoke.

With a sudden move, Mike stood up, the chair spinning away from him as he moved swiftly to her. Reflexively she took a step backward, meeting the door she'd entered.

He caught her to him. "Sweetheart," he murmured, his voice husky. "Oh, God, honey." Whatever had happened to make him glad to see her, it was good to be held close. Her cheek pressed against the buttons of the short-sleeved blue uniform shirt, the unyielding metal of his belt buckle biting into her ribs.

Gripping her shoulders, he pushed her back enough to look down into her upturned face. "How did you get here?" Her glance locked with his, and she couldn't say a word.

"Joy." She was pulled back against his chest, his fingers fastened in her hair, his cheek resting on the top of her head. He was shaking.

They stood that way for what seemed an eternity, her thoughts racing, trying to unscramble what was happening. From her locked-in view, she saw Ski move to stand near them.

He touched Mike's arm. "Let her go so she can talk to us," he told him.

Mike loosened his hold on her enough that she could look up at him by tilting her head. There were tears on his cheeks. She had dropped the small handbag, and now she raised her hands to touch his wet face.

"What's wrong? Why are you acting like this?"

His big hands came from her hair to frame her face. "When did you leave the hotel in Indianapolis?"

"My flight left at seven o'clock."

He closed his eyes tightly for an instant and shook his head. "You don't have a radio in your car?"

"I didn't turn it on." She tried to pull away but he

held on to her. She looked at Ski. "Tell me what's going on."

He managed a grin, but his eyes still showed an expression bordering on horror. "There was an explosion and fire at the hotel where you were staying. We didn't know you'd left."

"Mike?" Her eyes were wide as she looked at the anguish in his face as he continued to hold her.

"Come sit over here, honey." His voice was husky, and he swallowed several times. He led her to a chair near where he'd been sitting when she entered the room.

"Turn that thing off, Ski," he said, nodding toward the television playing in the corner of the room.

She glanced at the television screen to see smoke boiling upward, people screaming, giving the appearance of an explosion of fierce velocity, resembling a war movie.

"Everything all right, sergeant?" The policeman who directed her to the station dayroom stood in the door, curiosity on his face as he saw Sergeant Gresham with his arms around a young woman, the stranger who'd asked directions earlier.

Ski answered him. "Everything's great now, Roth."

The man withdrew after one more glance at the couple staring into each other's eyes, unaware of anything else that was going on in the room. He closed the door quietly behind him.

Mike knelt in front of her, holding both her hands so tightly it hurt, but she didn't attempt to withdraw them. She was fascinated by the drawn, hurt look on his face. Her heart went out to him for having to go through such anguish, thinking she was in the accident, an accident about which she knew nothing.

"Tonight, around dinnertime, there was an explosion at your hotel. The dining room was full of people, as was the ballroom where they planned to have a dance later."

She stared at him still without speaking, envisioning the glass and stone wonder she'd lived in all week, coming and going over the walkways, through the dining room dozens of times. She froze.

After a few seconds, he went on. "The exact number of casualties isn't known yet, but first reports indicate there will be many of them."

He looked down at their clasped hands before he went on. "We were watching the ten o'clock news and heard about it." He shuddered. "We thought you were still there."

"How did you know where I was staying?" That was the only thing that penetrated.

"I wanted to talk to you and had called Tom earlier in the week to see if he had a telephone number where you could be reached." He smiled a little, but his eyes were dark with feeling.

"You didn't call." She'd waited for him to call her, but he hadn't.

He shook his head. "I tried a couple of times, but you were always out." He stopped and brought her fingers up to brush them across his lips. "Finally I lost my nerve." He searched her face, his gaze going from her dark hair, over wide blue eyes, to parted lips.

He kissed her lightly before he went on, watching her blink at his touch. "I found out something you tried to tell me a long time ago. When you get struck down unexpectedly, it's pretty hard to be brave and strong, and quite easy to feel weak and helpless." He rubbed across her fingers with his thumbs. "I've never been so weak and helpless, and I was scared enough for six big, brave men."

"The accident? What did you say, Mike? Who were the people hurt?" She felt a blow in her middle as she suddenly remembered that some of the people she'd been with all week had planned to remain at the hotel overnight. Had she not been able to change her reservations she, too, would still have been there.

Weakness trembled through her already tired body, and she whispered, "Oh, my God!" She looked up at Ski as he stood helplessly by and back at the man holding on to her. "Oh, Mike."

He lifted her from the chair, gathering her to him to murmur reassuring words and stroke her hair as she trembled with reaction. "We don't know any names, and they won't release any before tomorrow, I'm sure." He looked down at her. "We'd better call Tom. He still thinks you're in Indianapolis."

He pushed her back into the chair and went to the desk, picking up the phone to dial. After a brief pause, he said, "Hello, Tom. Joy's here. She took an earlier plane." He waited, all the while watching her as she sat, dazed, thinking about her narrow escape.

"Yes. A little shaken up, but she's all right for the moment." He smiled at her, but her expression didn't change from the shock she felt. "Just a moment. Joy, he wants to hear you say you're okay."

He moved the phone close enough that she could take the receiver. "Joy?" Tom's voice was choked as he questioned her. "Tell me you're all right."

"Yes, I'm fine, Tom. I was going to wait until tomorrow to call you."

"Why did you leave early?" he asked, still looking for assurance that she was really safe.

"Mr. LeGrange was called to New York for a meeting, and we worked straight through today to finish up everything and skip the luncheon they planned for Saturday. I was able to change my reservations to tonight and left early."

"Thank God," Tom said, and she could feel the intense emotion in his voice. She looked at Mike, who was kneeling close by her chair, his arms around her as she talked. Her smile was uncertain, shock keeping her body stiff.

In answer to Tom's repeated question, she said, "Yes, I'll be fine. I don't understand what happened. Some of our friends may still be at the hotel. If you hear anything..." Her voice trailed off.

"Yes, Joy, if I hear anything I'll call," he promised. "Get some rest if you can." They said good night and hung up.

Mike caught her as she stood up and swayed. Her arms went around him, holding tightly. After a long time, she moved to look up at him. "You were crying?" she asked, her voice full of wonder.

"Yes," he said.

She smiled, her fingers resting on his chin. "I'm sorry. It isn't a nice feeling to be frightened."

"No," he admitted.

"Why don't you take her home, Mike," Ski interrupted them. "We're off duty now."

Mike drew in a sharp breath. "All right. Let's go, Joy." He looked at Ski. "If you need me anytime before noon tomorrow, call me at her apartment."

He was holding on to Joy's arm as he looked down at her. She didn't argue with him or ask for an explanation as they walked to her car. He took her keys silently and got behind the wheel. She didn't fasten the seat belt but slid across to sit near him as he guided the car through late-night traffic to her apartment. He took her bag from the trunk and held her as they walked through the empty foyer to her door, unlocking it with the key on her car ring.

Inside, he left her in the middle of the living room to place her bag in the bedroom and came back, stopping three feet in front of her to gaze silently. He held out his arms, and she walked into them, holding him tightly for a long time. Turning, he drew her with him to the couch and they sat quietly, his arms tight around her.

Then Mike spoke. "There's so much to say, Joy, I don't know where to start." Moving one hand to turn her chin to him, he kissed her cheek. "Perhaps by saying I love you?"

The dimples flashed and she nodded.

"I didn't call you Sunday because we didn't get into the office till midnight. Early Monday morning, they called an emergency meeting for our entire troop. I was the center of attention at that time because the captain and police commissioner were offering me a choice of nine-to-five jobs and not giving me much chance to turn any of them down."

He gave her a quick kiss. "Are you up to hearing all this?"

She nodded.

"When I called Conan's on Tuesday, you were already gone." He hesitated. "I walked the floor a good bit before I asked Tom for your phone number at the conference. I called Wednesday and Thursday, but you were always out."

She breathed out noisily. "We had long meetings, sometimes going over into the evenings."

He nodded. "By Friday morning, I'd lost my nerve and decided we'd discuss it together when you came home."

"Discuss what?"

"Honey," he whispered and kissed her on the mouth. She wanted to be held tightly and moved closer to him, her lips parting beneath the fierceness of his kisses. The warm tenderness of his arms holding her close, his mouth seeking possessively, started her blood racing and brought a gasp from her as he released her.

He was breathing unevenly as he said, "I found out that the empty spot in my life needs to be filled. I found out that only you can fill it for me."

"What if I'm not brave and strong, Mike? I don't know how I'd react if I knew you were in real danger at any given time." Her voice was a mere whisper. "If I'm human enough to love you with all my heart, how can I deny I'd always react like a human being?"

"I think I'd like having you worry about me." His fingers tightened on her arms. "Our weaknesses together will be enough strength to endure anything as long as we're together."

Her tired sigh wasn't lost on Mike. He picked her up and took her to the bedroom, where he placed her gently on the spread. He worked silently, undressing her, reaching behind him to the chest to take out her favorite T-shirt, giving it barely a glance as he pulled it over her head, easing the sheet over her, tucking it in.

"Is there any of the cognac left?" he asked.

"A little. In the china cabinet."

In a moment he was back with only one glass almost filled with amber-colored liquid over ice. He held it to her lips. "Drink this."

Mike sat by her on the bed until a soft warm glow from the alcohol relaxed her. She was dimly aware of his body coming to rest against hers, of arms enfolding her, of his brief kiss.

The last sound she heard was Mike saying, "Darling."

Chapter Nineteen

Her hand searched the bed beside her before she opened her eyes. When it found empty space, she gave a startled cry and sat up.

"Mike?"

He turned from the window at the first sound she made and hurried across the room to kneel beside the bed. He wore only his uniform pants, his bare shoulders gleaming in the dimness of the room.

"I thought you'd left me." Joy's voice had the softness of a child's accusing him of desertion.

"Never." His hands were gentle, petting her, rubbing her arms. "I made coffee. Want some?"

"Yes." The nightmare of the night before came back and she opened her mouth to question him, her eyes afraid to ask.

His fingers came against her lips. "Later."

She had spent the night in Mike's arms, aware that he held her as sleep came quickly on top of the cognac he made her drink. Sometime during the night, she had twisted with her dreams, and Mike's quiet voice reassuring her, his arms holding her close to him, coaxed her awake from the disturbing shadows and back to sleep. Several times she felt his lips on her cheek, brushing her hair, but there were no demands on her even when she rolled close to cling to him.

Now she pulled him down to her, seeking the warmth of his lips, and felt the tremor go through him. With open mouth she kissed him, tasting the mint from his toothpaste as she slid her tongue across his lips. She heard him gasp and thrust her tongue deep into the moistness he opened for her.

Exploring hands went to her waist, shoving at her shirt. It went up and Mike's hands skimmed her belly, over her hips, searching, until he found the firmness of breasts loose beneath the material.

Somehow she was naked, achingly aware of Mike's hard-muscled body pressed demandingly against her. His mouth roamed her face, her throat, her shoulders, lingering over the hardened rose-brown peaks lifted to him, his tongue roughly massaging them until she moaned. There was no part of her he didn't touch; every inch of her body was alive and begging for his gentle kisses. Every spot he kissed, she held his head until he moved away from her to search out another delectable bit of her to taste, to nibble, to lick. And then there was no more time to wait, no more hesitating, no more denial.

He pulled her up onto his body and she looked down into his face. A light sheen of perspiration gathered on his forehead, and he breathed hard through parted lips. She kissed him, feeling his hands urge her hips downward as he forced himself into her. He gave a soft cry of satisfaction against her mouth and lay still, his arms tightening to keep her from moving.

Moments passed and she lay there, content to be in Mike's arms, completely in his possession. His moaning sigh against her mouth signaled the end of his resistance. Pure pleasure overwhelmed her as their bodies engaged in a fierce exercise, escalating them into an explosion of greedy passion that rocked their very souls.

"BE CAREFUL, Joy, it's hot," Mike said as he handed her a cup of coffee. She had taken a shower and put on a short cotton robe, sitting on the couch with her feet tucked beneath her. Her smile was dreamy as she met Mike's dark gray eyes.

The smile faded at his serious expression when he sat beside her. "We have to talk."

She waited. "The casualties in the hotel fire have been accounted for. No one Tom knew was listed."

She drew in a tremulous breath and whispered, "Oh, Mike."

He nodded. "Now about us." He reached for the cup and placed it on the table, then picked up both her hands. "Do you remember all I said last night?"

"Every word. Are you sure, Mike?"

He shook his head. "Not about everything."

She stiffened and tried to withdraw her hands. "If you didn't mean—"

He took back her hands. "About us, our love for

From This Day

each other, that I don't intend to live without you...
those are certainties. I had a few misgivings about the
job, but I thought we'd talk about it and decide.''

The love she had for him at that moment threatened to overcome everything, and she wanted to
throw her arms around him and tell him they could
conquer it all. Instead she asked quietly, "Can you
adjust to coming home at five o'clock every day and
no calls during the night?"

He leaned over to nuzzle her cheek. "I've never
had you to come home to, but I think it's worth a
try." He bent closer to stare directly into her questioning eyes. "I love you in orange more than in gray.
You'll have to order some more of the Tigers shirts."

Hot color stained her face and he laughed, gathering her to him again, and they remained close together as the minutes ticked away.

"Honey?"

"Yes, Mike."

"What about Ken?"

She leaned back to look into his eyes. A tiny smile
lifted the corners of his mouth, but the gray of his
eyes watched her closely, no smile in them.

"Ken has been gone a long time, Mike. He left long
before I even knew it, and when I realized I was
alone, it was no longer as frightening as I'd thought it
would be." She wanted to coax a smile into his eyes to
warm the gray, to light it with the love she wanted
from him. "He's not a question anymore."

The smile was slow in coming, but when it did, it
was everything she'd hoped for. They clung to each

other until he pulled away once more and smiled down at her.

"I want to take you home with me to meet my mother."

"Does she know about me?"

"Yes." His voice was reassuring.

"How much?"

"You're the only one I've ever called her up to talk about. The only one I've ever shown her a picture of. The only one I've asked her to invite to Denver for a weekend as soon as you agree to go."

Almost breathless, she asked, "Where did you get a picture of me?"

"There was a big write-up in the *Nevada State Journal* when you went to the open house for the Ridenhour shindig, and a beautiful picture of you, dimples and all." He kissed her briefly on the mouth. "I sent it to Mother, and she called me as soon as she got it."

"Why did she call you about a picture of a woman she'd never seen before?"

"Because she was suspicious."

"Suspicious? Of what?"

"I told you. I've never wanted her to meet anyone I dated before. I also hinted that I might take the promotion they've been dangling in front of me for years, and then she knew I was serious." He smiled suddenly. "By the way, will you marry me?" When she continued to look into his eyes, he whispered, "I need you. Will you take all kinds of chances with me? Do you love me enough to stay with me forever, however long that might be?"

For a moment longer she stared, then smiled, the dimples appearing as her tongue touched the crooked front tooth an instant before his mouth descended to cover hers. A familiar warm thrill slithered along her spine, to the bottom of her stomach, through her thighs, and she pressed closer to him, her body moving gently into the shape of his.

"Forever, Mike," she said against his mouth. "Forever, from this day."

You're invited to accept 4 books and a surprise gift Free!

Acceptance Card

Mail to: **Harlequin Reader Service®**

In the U.S.	In Canada
2504 West Southern Ave.	P.O. Box 2800, Postal Station A
Tempe, AZ 85282	5170 Yonge Street
	Willowdale, Ontario M2N 6J3

YES! Please send me 4 free Harlequin American Romance® novels and my free surprise gift. Then send me 4 brand new novels as they come off the presses. Bill me at the low price of $2.25 each —an 11% saving off the retail price. There are no shipping, handling or other hidden costs. There is no minimum number of books I must purchase. I can always return a shipment and cancel at any time. Even if I never buy another book from Harlequin, the 4 free novels and the surprise gift are mine to keep forever.

154 BPA-BPGE

Name _____ (PLEASE PRINT)

Address _____ Apt. No. _____

City _____ State/Prov. _____ Zip/Postal Code _____

This offer is limited to one order per household and not valid to present subscribers. Price is subject to change.

ACAR-SUB-1

Readers rave about
Harlequin American Romance!

"...the best series of modern romances
I have read...great, exciting, stupendous,
wonderful."
  —S.E.* Coweta, Oklahoma

"...they are absolutely fantastic...going to be
a smash hit and hard to keep on the
bookshelves."
  —P.D., Easton, Pennsylvania

"The American line is great. I've enjoyed
every one I've read so far."
  —W.M.K., Lansing, Illinois

"...the best stories I have read in a long
time."
  —R.H., Northport, New York

*Names available on request.

You're invited to accept 4 books and a surprise gift Free!

Acceptance Card

Mail to: Harlequin Reader Service®

In the U.S.
2504 West Southern Ave.
Tempe, AZ 85282

In Canada
P.O. Box 2800, Postal Station A
5170 Yonge Street
Willowdale, Ontario M2N 6J3

YES! Please send me 4 free Harlequin Temptation® novels and my free surprise gift. Then send me 4 brand new novels every month as they come off the presses. Bill me at the low price of $1.99 each ($1.95 in Canada)—a 13% saving off the retail price. There are no shipping, handling or other hidden costs. There is no minimum number of books I must purchase. I can always return a shipment and cancel at any time. Even if I never buy another book from Harlequin, the 4 free novels and the surprise gift are mine to keep forever.

142 BPX-BPGE

Name _____ (PLEASE PRINT)

Address _____ Apt. No. _____

City _____ State/Prov. _____ Zip/Postal Code _____